Praise for the Novels
of Cassie Edwards

"Edwards consistently gives the reader a strong love story, rich in Indian lore, filled with passion and memorable characters. . . . Wonderful, unforgettable."
—*Romantic Times*

"Unique . . . a romantic tale." —*Midwest Book Review*

"Edwards puts an emphasis on placing authentic customs and language in each book. Her Indian books have generated much interest throughout the country, and elsewhere." —*Journal Gazette* (Mattoon, IL)

"Cassie Edwards is known for her exciting, sensual Native American romances. . . . This novel is a winner." —*Affaire de Coeur*

"A fine writer . . . accurate. . . . Indian history and language keep readers interested."
—*Greeley Tribune* (Greeley, CO)

"Captivating . . . heartwarming . . . beautiful . . . a winner." —*Rendezvous*

"Edwards moves readers with love and compassion."
—*Bell, Book & Candle*

RUNNING FOX

Lakota

Cassie Edwards

A SIGNET BOOK

SIGNET
Published by New American Library, a division of
Penguin Group (USA) Inc., 375 Hudson Street,
New York, New York 10014, USA
Penguin Group (Canada), 90 Eglinton Avenue East, Suite 700, Toronto,
Ontario M4P 2Y3, Canada (a division of Pearson Penguin Canada Inc.)
Penguin Books Ltd., 80 Strand, London WC2R 0RL, England
Penguin Ireland, 25 St. Stephen's Green, Dublin 2,
Ireland (a division of Penguin Books Ltd.)
Penguin Group (Australia), 250 Camberwell Road, Camberwell, Victoria 3124,
Australia (a division of Pearson Australia Group Pty. Ltd.)
Penguin Books India Pvt. Ltd., 11 Community Centre, Panchsheel Park,
New Delhi - 110 017, India
Penguin Group (NZ), cnr Airborne and Rosedale Roads, Albany,
Auckland 1310, New Zealand (a division of Pearson New Zealand Ltd.)
Penguin Books (South Africa) (Pty.) Ltd., 24 Sturdee Avenue,
Rosebank, Johannesburg 2196, South Africa

Penguin Books Ltd., Registered Offices:
80 Strand, London WC2R 0RL, England

First published by Signet, an imprint of New American Library,
a division of Penguin Group (USA) Inc.

First Printing, December 2006
10 9 8 7 6 5 4 3 2 1

In appreciation and with fondness, I dedicate *Running Fox*, the first book of my new Dream-catcher series, to my editor, Claire Zion, and to Tina Brown, assistant editor.

Cassie Edwards

My Running Fox,
Named for your quickness, your cunning.
Smart fox, you are,
Hunting, for need, to feed,
Deceiving all by far.
Oh, fox, how so cunning, clever, you are,
My Running Fox.
All that you have been through,
I will be smarter than you.
I will find you.
We will be foxes to share a love so true.
                    —Modestia M. York

The life of an Indian is like the wings of the air. That is why you notice the hawk knows how to get his prey. The Indian is like that. The hawk swoops down on its prey; so does the Indian. In his lament, he is like an animal. For instance, the coyote is sly; so is the Indian. The eagle is the same. That is why the Indian is always feathered up; he is a relative to the wings of the air.

—Black Elk, Oglala Sioux Holy Man

Chapter 1

Michigan . . . 1879
The Moon of Sore Eyes—March

The spring fur hunters had been fortunate, and a heavy winter had produced much maple sugar for the Fox Band of the Lakota tribe. They were now busy harvesting the sugar from the maple trees near their village.

The sky was calm and blue.

Water gurgled peacefully over rust-colored cobblestones in a close-by shallow stream.

A bark sugar house stood in the midst of the maple grove. A long fire burned in the house, where brass kettles were suspended in a row over the blaze.

Outside, little troughs of basswood and birchen

basins had been made to receive the sweet drops, the life's blood of the trees.

The sound of horses' hooves made Chief Running Fox realize that someone was approaching. He knew who it was without even looking.

It was Joseph Brock, known to everyone in the area as Whiskey Joe, a man who peddled the seductive poison whiskey, always attempting to trade it for the red man's expensive pelts.

A young chief of twenty-six winters, Running Fox was tall, muscled, and handsome, with sculpted facial features and long, flowing raven-black hair. Today he wore a coat made of bear fur over his thick fringed-buckskin outfit. The chief was angry at Whiskey Joe, who would not take no for an answer as he tried to sell his wares. The whiskey peddler persistently pestered Running Fox's people and those of other Indian villages in the area. Some villages tolerated the whiskey man, although most despised the mere sight of him.

Running Fox's people were about to be bothered again by the evil white man.

It was a known fact that he acquired pelts from the red man and then sold them later on the white market for much profit, taking that profit from the red man.

"*Iho, ho-iyaya-yo*, continue with the harvest," Running Fox said stiffly as he turned and gazed at his people, seeing the contempt for the whiskey peddler in all of their eyes. "I will again send the evil man away. *Hoh*, one day he will finally realize that he wastes his time coming among us."

Running Fox watched them for a moment longer, as they resumed their maple syrup harvesting. Then he turned and waited for the whiskey peddler to arrive.

He soon saw the wagon and team of four horses as they came around a bend. Until now they had been hidden by a thick stand of cottonwood trees.

Whiskey Joe was not in the wagon alone, however. Besides the many kegs of whiskey behind him, he had once again brought his daughter with him. She sat dutifully at his right side, a blanket shared between them as it rested across their laps.

Running Fox tried not to pay heed to the beautiful *mitawin*, woman, but instead focused entirely on the problem at hand, although it was hard not to look at her when she was near. Each time he saw her, wonder of her pressed harder and harder on his heart.

Today, in one glance, even at this distance, he could see enough of her to marvel at her fiery red hair, which the fur hat she wore did not entirely cover. Her hat framed an oval, suntanned face, with long black lashes over eyes the color of violets. Her lips were shaped beautifully. . . .

No! He could not—would not—think any more

about the woman, who mesmerized him with her loveliness.

He had to think only about the whiskey peddler.

Over and over again Running Fox had ordered Whiskey Joe not to come among his people, for when the Lakota warriors, especially the young braves, drank the *minnewakan*, spirit water, they were known to do things they normally would not do. It made them become someone foreign to themselves and their Lakota people.

As the horses stopped a few feet from Running Fox, he stepped closer to the wagon. Eyes narrowed angrily, he gazed directly into the pale gray eyes of the whiskey peddler. The man wore a fur cape, and he had red hair, which hung down past his shoulders.

"*Iho*, you have been told never to come on our land again," Running Fox said tightly, his eyes warring with the peddler's. "Turn the wagon around. Go away and do not come again. One day you will press your luck too far and you will be met by many strung bows, the deadly arrows aimed at your heart."

He heard a gasp and knew that it came from the woman. She was more threatened by his words than the one for whom they were intended. It was obvious that the white man was not affected by the warning at all, for he did not move a muscle and again seemed not to have heard at all.

Running Fox gazed at the woman, and when he did he felt as he had the other times she had come with the whiskey peddler into his village. She was looking directly at him, yet didn't seem to truly see him. He always wondered about that, for he had learned long ago to read one's soul when he looked into their eyes. It was impossible to know this woman any better by looking into her eyes, when she seemed not to be looking into his.

Hai, this jarred his senses so much that he looked quickly away from her again.

"Whiskey man, if I have to tell you one more time to leave, it will be the last time you will ever receive a warning from anyone," Running Fox said, again in his even, gentle tone.

"Are you threatening me?" Joe gasped as the woman reached over and grabbed his hand.

Whiskey Joe felt her hand trembling and saw that she had gone pale from fear.

He then realized that he had gone as far as he could today in trying to make a deal with the stubborn savage.

He turned and glared at Running Fox, then snapped his reins. The horses made a wide turn, quickly taking Whiskey Joe and the woman away from the threat.

"You haven't heard the last from me!" Joe shouted over his shoulder. "No savage threatens me and gets away with it!"

Running Fox's lips curled into a slow smile. The whiskey man called the wrong man a savage. He was truly the savage, though his threats did not affect Running Fox whatsoever. Running Fox knew that even the white community did not approve of what the whiskey man was doing, for they knew that if the peddler's *minnewakan* was drunk by too many red men, the whites could be the ones who suffered because of it. It was a known fact that there was something about the spirit water that made the young warriors and braves turn into someone different from their normal selves. There seemed to be something in the spirit water that burned clean through into their souls!

Running Fox's thoughts were interrupted when he saw a horse approaching and recognized it to be his scout, whose job it was to keep an eye on what was happening in the community, both the white villages and the neighboring Lakota and Chippewa villages.

He ran to meet Wind Eagle halfway.

Wind Eagle drew a tight rein and stopped, his eyes revealing a deep pain that made Running Fox afraid. The news could be nothing but bad!

"*Iho*, my chief, I bring you news of the death of two young Chippewa braves," Wind Eagle said, dismounting. He stood eye to eye with Running Fox. "The youths partook of too much *minnewakan*. They drank themselves to death, and another young brave of that same band, whose mind was warped by the spirit water, raped a beautiful young maiden of his own band—his cousin!"

"Which band of Chippewa?" Running Fox asked, anger hot inside his chest.

"Our old *toka*, enemy, the Yellow Feather Band," Wind Eagle said, his voice drawn.

Running Fox hung his head, slowly shook it back and forth, then looked into Wind Eagle's eyes again. *"Ei-i-i,"* he said, his way of voicing regret. "The Yellow Feather Band is known to have ordered Whiskey Joe not to come into their village."

"It is said that Whiskey Joe met with the young braves away from the village and made a deal with them that became deadly," Wind Eagle said, his voice tight.

Running Fox was both saddened and enraged by the news. It tore at his very being. "Go back to our village," he said. "I will bring our warriors. We will go into council and make decisions about what to do about what has happened."

Wind Eagle nodded, mounted his steed, wheeled it around, and rode the short distance to the village as Running Fox spoke to his warriors.

The women and children were left behind to continue the harvest while Running Fox and his warriors met in their large council house, where a fire was kept burning at all times for such sudden meetings.

Running Fox stood before his warriors and shared the news brought to him by Wind Eagle, causing the hatred for the whiskey peddler to worsen among them all.

"We must find a way to keep this from happening to one of our young braves," Running Fox said, his fringed buckskins tight on his muscled body.

"But we cannot out and out kill the whiskey peddler," one of his warriors said. "That would only bring trouble to our village from the white authorities. We cannot allow this to happen."

"No, we cannot," Running Fox said. He stared into the flames of the fire.

He thought for a moment, then smiled from warrior to warrior. "I have a perfect plan," he said, telling them exactly how it would be done.

He shared his plan with them. Then he proposed a backup strategy, in case the plan failed.

"But, my chief, there is much danger in what you suggest," Wind Eagle said solemnly. "Are you certain you wish to do something as bold as that? The whiskey peddler will surely realize it was our band who did this."

"The whiskey peddler will not be able to tell which particular band did this deed, for he has made enemies with many in this area—Lakota and Chippewa," Running Fox said, his eyes gleaming. "He has caused both tribes many problems from the sale of his spirit water, often trading to the young behind their parents' backs, for all young braves are good hunters and have expensive pelts for trade."

"That is true," Wind Eagle said, nodding.

"No one will know who did this against the evil man, and even if these plans do not work, I have one last idea that will terrify the man so much that he will stop trading whiskey altogether!"

"But, my chief," another warrior argued, "the whiskey peddler knows that the Lakota's hands are tied, that the white authorities can do anything they wish to our Lakota people and no one would interfere should they realize it is our band who does something to the evil white man."

"If it comes to that, all bands could come together, Lakota and Chippewa," Running Fox said stiffly. "As one force, we Lakota and Chippewa outnumber the whites in the area."

"I do not want war," the same warrior said. "I want to be able to hunt without having to watch my back."

"Most whites are cowards," Running Fox reassured his warriors. "They talk big and at the same time shudder in their boots in the presence of a red man."

All the warriors finally agreed with Running Fox about what must be done, and how.

He could hardly wait to initiate the plans, for one of these proposals benefited him personally, in more ways than one!

Chapter 2

"Naughty Nancy!" the unruly crowd of men shouted as Nancy was helped from the stage by her mother, Carole.

Tears streamed from Nancy's eyes over the added humiliation of having to sing before the drunken men, let alone having been nicknamed something so ugly by them when she was anything but naughty.

And she couldn't see one inch ahead of her without her eyeglasses.

But she had been told by her stepfather that she had to perform without them, because she was much prettier that way.

In the long run, she had decided that she was better off without the eyeglasses anyway, because without them she couldn't see the ugly drunks who frequented the theater with lust in their eyes as they gaped openly at her.

The shouts continued behind Nancy.

She cringed.

"Mama, just listen to them," she cried, stumbling along as her mother guided her farther away from the stage. "Why can't they stop calling me such a filthy name? It's . . . it's . . . disgusting."

"Just ignore them, honey," Carole murmured, as she led Nancy toward her dressing room.

"I hate it, Mama," Nancy cried as the shouts continued behind her. "I hate your husband! Why do you go along with him, forcing me to do these things that I don't want to do? He not only makes me accompany him on his whiskey runs, but I also have to sing in his terrible establishment."

"Why? Because he is my husband," Carole said, grabbing Nancy when she stumbled over a prop that she had not seen.

Even though deep down inside herself, Carole did not approve of how her daughter was being treated by Joe, she nevertheless found her husband's theater, the Crystal Palace, beautiful, with its lavish decorations and red velvet everywhere. It was the entertainment spot of Dry Gulch, even though it was a known fact that most respectable ladies would not enter, fearing the worst from the men who frequented it.

The building was one and a half stories high. It

had two main rooms—a saloon where a man could enjoy a five-dollar bottle of champagne or pay a mere one dollar for a shot of whiskey, and a theater section.

The balconies in the theater were divided into boxes that ran the full length of both sides.

The most unruly men sat in the boxes, where they could get a better look at Nancy as she sang.

"How could you have married such a man?" Nancy cried, reaching out and feeling her way on to her dressing room, trying not to trip.

"And, Mama, how could you make me do something I loathe?" Nancy continued. "I . . . hate . . . performing before those filthy-minded men. I hate going with Joe on the whiskey runs."

"But, darling, forget everything except your beautiful voice and how I am so proud of it, and you," Carole said.

She led Nancy on into the dressing room, which was awash with light from a crystal chandelier that hung at the center of the room.

"And just look at you, Nancy," Carole said. "You are so beautiful and stylish. That silk gown with its marten trim is exquisite on you."

Nancy slammed the door behind her and slapped her mother's hand away as her mother began fussing with the fur.

"Mama, just quit it," Nancy cried. She began feeling around the dressing table, knocking over a bottle of imported perfume. Her mother quickly grabbed the bottle to save as much as she could, since it was expensive and had come directly from France just for Nancy to wear during her performances.

"Mama, where are my eyeglasses?" Nancy said, getting more frustrated by the minute.

"Here, darling," Carole said, gently placing Nancy's eyeglasses on the bridge of her nose. "Now, Nancy, take a look in the mirror and see how pretty you are with those flowers in your hair. That's why Joe wants you to sing for him, not just because you have the best voice in these whole United States."

Nancy reached up and yanked the flowers from her hair, tossing them to the floor and angrily stamping on them. "I hate it all," she cried. "I want to leave, Mama. Please, oh, please, let's leave."

Carole's eyes wavered, one of her hands moving nervously down her own stylish dress, which accentuated her figure at her age of forty. "And where would you suggest we go?" she said.

She flipped her golden hair back from her shoulders, her green eyes wavering as she met Nancy's gaze. Her daughter's eyes were such a pretty violet color that they sometimes mesmerized a man to speechlessness.

They seemed even more accentuated now since Joe had forced Nancy to dye her black hair red. The violet contrasted so invitingly with the red.

Carole hadn't wanted to have anything to do with Nancy dyeing her hair that nasty red color, but Joe had demanded it be done. He had said that red hair would make Nancy even more entrancing to the gentlemen who frequented his theater, for, as Joe had said, all men saw redheaded women as more passionate than other women.

Nancy turned and glared at the closed door, visibly shuddering. "Do you hear it, Mama?" she cried, framing her own face with her hands in frustration. "The men are still shouting 'Naughty Nancy.' They are so wrong to call me that. I have done nothing indecent, ever, to earn the name. It sickens me, Mama. Just sickens me."

"It's an honor that they continue to chant that, Nancy," Carole said, clasping her hands together before her and sighing. "It means they like you and want you to come back out there to sing again. Go on, Nancy. Why don't you go out and sing one more song for them?"

She started to take the eyeglasses from Nancy's nose so that the girl could return to the stage, but Nancy slapped her hands away.

"Never," she said.

"I wouldn't say never, Nancy," Carole said nervously. "You know that you have to do another performance tonight before you can go to your room."

Nancy turned and gazed into the mirror again. She ran a hand slowly down one of her cheeks. "I'm becoming someone I don't know," she sobbed. "And all because of my stepfather."

She turned on her heel and glared at her mother. "I loathe him," she said tightly. "Not only because of what he's doing to me and you, but also because of how he treats the Indians. He is so loathsome when he goes to the villages with his whiskey even though he is not welcome there. And how dare he continue to make me go with him!"

"You must go with him," Carole said, stepping up next to Nancy and staring at her own image in the mirror, her fingers following a path of wrinkles that ran from the corners of her eyes. "It's your pretty hair and eyes that help distract the Indians so much they forget the bad of the whiskey."

"It didn't help distract one Indian chief today," Nancy said, tilting her chin stubbornly. "It was wonderful how he stood up to Joe." She smiled. "I wish I could have seen the Indian's face when he ordered Joe away. Ah, his voice. If he looks anything like his voice makes him sound, he must be quite a handsome young chief."

"Stop talking like that," Carole said, gasping. "You shouldn't be thinking about Indians at all, much less be glad that one got the best of Joe today."

"Mama, I just don't like thinking that if the Indians do buy Joe's rotgut, I might be partially to blame for whatever the younger braves do if they get intoxicated," she said, shuddering. "They are easily duped into trading for the whiskey. I have seen more than once how the young braves go behind their parents' backs, even their chief's, to hunt and use the pelts to trade for whiskey."

She sighed heavily. "There were three of them recently who traded for the rotgut Joe so eagerly handed to them in those jugs," she murmured. "I knew they were young because Joe told me so after we left. I had suspected it from the sound of their voices. They were young braves whose voices were just turning into sounding more adult."

Nancy's eyes gleamed. "I should wear my eyeglasses the next time I am forced to go with Joe to the Indian villages," she snapped angrily. "Surely I'd scare the Indians away, for they don't know what eyeglasses are, do they?"

"No, I doubt that they do," Carole said, "but don't count on your father letting you wear your eyeglasses when you go on the whiskey runs—not ever."

"*Step*father," Nancy corrected. "He'll never be a father to me."

Nancy ran her fingers through her hair as she again gazed into the mirror. "Mama, I sometimes feel so defenseless without my eyeglasses on," she murmured. "If the Indians decided to shoot me and Joe, I'd not know it until I heard the report of the gun and felt the bullet pierce my flesh."

"Don't talk like that," Carole gasped. She picked up a brush and tried to brush Nancy's hair, but stopped when Nancy shoved her hand away.

Nancy turned and gazed into her mother's eyes. "Also, Mama, I feel defenseless because no one has taught me how to shoot a gun or how to ride a horse. But even without the knowledge of those two things, I still must find a way to flee this life that gets worse by the day."

"Nancy, stop saying such nonsense," Carole said, then swung around, paling, when Joe came into the room, staring first at her, then at Nancy, his fists on his hips.

"What's going on here?" he asked, forking an eyebrow. "An Indian parley?"

He laughed throatily. Then, when neither Nancy nor Carole seemed eager to respond to him, he waited a moment longer to pursue the question as he took a cigar from his gold-brocade vest pocket.

He licked one end preparatory to lighting up his fragrant Havana.

Today he was dressed expensively, and his long red hair was drawn back from his face and tied in a neat ponytail.

"Honey," Carole said, finally receptive to him after having been startled by his sudden appearance.

She went to him and gave him a hug, shuddering when he shoved her away and lit the cigar and blew smoke into her face.

"I asked what's going on," Joe said. He looked from Carole to Nancy again. "Cat got your tongues, or what?"

"Nothing is going on, Joe," Carole said, sidling up next to him again.

She tried to hide her shudder of disgust when he swept an arm around her waist.

She despised Joe as much as Nancy did, but she had nowhere else to go, so she had to tolerate him and all the vileness he had brought into the marriage.

"Just girl talk, Joe," Carole said. "Just girl talk."

"Girl talk, huh?" Joe said, his pale gray eyes narrowing as he glared at Nancy. "Is that true, Nancy dearest? Is that all that's going on here?"

"Honey, Nancy is just tired after her performance, that's all," Carole said, feeling his arm tighten around her and realizing he wasn't happy with her explanation.

"Well, Naughty Nancy, you'd best get rested up real quick-like, then," Joe snarled. "The men are antsy as they wait for your second performance of the night."

He stepped away from Carole. He yanked the eyeglasses away from Nancy. "I hate those things," he said. "I oughtta break 'em so you'd never put 'em on again."

A quick panic filled Nancy. She forced a smile as she reached for the eyeglasses. "You don't mean it," she murmured. "Please give them to me, Joe. You know I need them."

"Well, yeah, I guess so," Joe said. He shrugged and gave them back to her. "But don't put 'em on. You're wanted out there, Nancy. Hear your audience calling for you?"

Nancy stiffened as she heard the men chanting, *"Naughty Nancy, we want Naughty Nancy,"* over and over again.

"Do it," Joe commanded. He nodded toward Carole. "Help her out there, wife. Now. Not later."

Carole took Nancy's eyeglasses from her and laid them on the dressing table, then placed a gentle arm around her daughter's waist. "Come on, dear," she said. "One more performance tonight and that'll be all until tomorrow."

Nancy sent a glare at Joe over her shoulder as she left the room. Although she couldn't see the rascal's reaction, she grew more determined than ever to find a way to escape this horrible life!

Joe caught up with her just before she went out on the stage. "You forgot something," he said, replacing the fresh flowers in her hair. He stood back and beamed. "Now ain't you a picture of prettiness?"

Nancy sighed, then walked with her mother out onto the stage.

The wolf whistles caused her spine to stiffen.

But as soon as she began singing, everything and everyone got quiet.

For a moment or two, Nancy could forget where she was, and what she was doing, and why.

She did love to sing!

But she would much rather be singing to a baby. Oh, how badly she did wish to find a man who would take her away from this sort of life.

To be a wife and mother was her true dream!

Chapter 3

The temperatures had warmed considerably over-
night. The birds were welcoming the warmer air
with song.

Nancy sat stiffly beside her stepfather on another
whiskey run. She found today incredibly surreal
compared to yesterday. Chief Running Fox was actually friendly and had even invited her stepfather
back to his village with his whiskey.

She wished she had her eyeglasses on so that she
could see into Running Fox's eyes. She surely
would be able to see his mood and decide whether
or not his cheerfulness was real or fake.

She was so afraid that he was fooling her stepfather.

If so, she dreaded what might transpire next.

"I don't know what changed your mind, but I'm

appreciative of it," Joe said as he watched Running
Fox's warriors take the last jugs of whiskey from
the back of his wagon.

He couldn't believe his luck.

This was the most generous of all the chiefs he
had dealt with.

Running Fox had actually given him ten of those
plush pelts for each jug of whiskey.

That amounted to one hundred pelts for the ten
jugs he had handed over to the stupid savages.

If Running Fox knew how much money Joe
would get when he went to sell the pelts at market,
he'd probably scalp his own self over being this asi-
nine in his dealings with this whiskey peddler.

But when Running Fox's warriors had told Joe
that their chief had had a change of heart, mainly
because it had been a good hunting season, he
couldn't get his wagon loaded fast enough.

Running Fox stood by, silent, as the last of the
spirit water was taken from the evil man's wagon,
for Running Fox had something on his mind this
morning besides the *minnewakan*. There had been
another reason why he had wanted Whiskey Joe to
return to his village to be tricked.

The flame-haired white woman, Whiskey Joe's
daughter, was that reason.

He wanted to get a better look at her.

The fact that Whiskey Joe had come so eagerly
with his spirit water after having been warned

against selling it, was proof enough that the white man didn't have any concept of right and wrong.

It proved that he was a man of little intelligence, for if it had been Running Fox being asked back into a village after having been ordered away so often, he would have had the brains to realize he was being duped!

But as it was, the whiskey man would get his first lesson of what it meant to use one's brain more effectively.

If today's lesson didn't convince him that Running Fox meant everything that he had said, the next lesson would include the man's flame-haired daughter.

"Well, that's that," Joe said, beaming. "We've made a good trade here today, Chief Running Fox. Let me know when you run out of whiskey again." He chuckled. His eyes gleamed. "I've more where that came from."

"I am certain that you do," Running Fox said, turning his eyes back to the whiskey peddler.

"I thank you a bunch for the pelts," Joe said. He grabbed his horse's reins. "Like I said, let me know when you need more whiskey. I'll be back here with more before you can bat an eye."

He chuckled to himself and started to turn his team of horses and wagon around in order to leave, but stopped and went pale when he saw several warriors taking the whiskey to the nearby creek, and beginning to pour it, a jug at a time, into the water.

"What the—?" Joe gasped, stunned speechless and mortified by what was happening. All of the whiskey he had just traded for the plush robes was now in the creek and floating away over the rocks, a sparkling color of gold in the sun's glow.

"Why in hell did you do that?" Joe shrieked. He started to jump from the wagon but stopped when Running Fox came and placed a hand flat on his chest.

Nancy felt faint. She knew that something had just gone terribly wrong, but did not know what.

"Joe, what's wrong?" she choked out, flinching when her stepfather let out a cry of pain beside her.

"Chief, you're hurting me," Joe yelled. "Let go of my wrist. What's going on here? Let . . . go. Let me go! I want no more part of what you're doing."

Then Joe's voice went flat. "And if you think you're going to take back those robes, you've got another think coming," he said. He grabbed the rifle he kept hidden beneath the lap blanket that he shared with Nancy as they traveled.

Joe screeched with pain.

"Lord—Lord—" Nancy cried.

"Give me back my firearm," Joe said, his voice tight and sober. "All I want is to leave. Do you hear? Leave!"

"After we take back what is ours," Running Fox said. He nodded toward several warriors.

Some came and stood around the wagon, arrows notched threateningly on their bowstrings, while others began taking the pelts from the wagon, piling them a few feet away.

"You can't—" Joe gasped out.

"*Ay-uh*, we can, and we are," Running Fox said, smiling smugly into the man's pale eyes. "You see, white man, today is a day of lessons for you. It is to teach you to heed warnings when they are given to you."

"What do you mean?" Joe said as the last pelt was taken from the wagon. He glared at his rifle, which Running Fox was holding.

"I warned you against selling your spirit water to people of my skin color," Running Fox said dryly. "Word was brought that you ignored the warning. Today is a lesson taught you that you can see, instead of mere warnings spoken aloud to you."

"But what you did is such a waste of good whiskey," Joe blurted.

"That is exactly why I did it," Running Fox said, slowly smiling at Whiskey Joe. "I see this as the only way to keep as many young braves as possible from the *minnewakan*, spirit water."

He stepped closer and glared at Whiskey Joe as he related the tragic story about the recent deaths of the young Chippewa braves and the rape of one of their young maidens.

"This all happened because of *minnewakan*," Running Fox said. His eyes moved slowly to the whiskey peddler's daughter. "It could have been your daughter who was raped."

Joe blanched as he looked at Nancy and saw how pale and afraid she was.

He glared at Running Fox. "Is that a threat against my daughter?" he asked. "You'd best never touch my Nancy. Do you hear?"

Nancy was trembling. She couldn't help but believe that she might be living her last moments on this earth, for it was evident that Running Fox was definitely toying with her stepfather.

She tried her best not to look afraid, but instead to appear courageous in the face of danger. Surely the young chief would appreciate courage in a woman and let her be!

She prayed so, anyhow!

"I have had enough of you today," Running Fox said, glowering into the white man's eyes. "Leave and never return, and hear me well when I say that you had best do your whiskey selling to whites, not to people of my skin color. I have done this today to show you a small example of how far I will go to stop your evil and to make you understand the importance of not allowing this evil to spread any further among the Indian community."

Running Fox stepped closer and spoke into Whiskey Joe's face. "If I ever hear that you have taken your spirit water to any more of the Lakota bands, who are linked by heart and blood to my own band, you will pay dearly for the mistake."

"You listen to me," Joe growled. "You are taking on more than you can chew."

Joe grew pale when the Lakota warriors inched closer with their notched bows.

He saw just how close the arrows were to him and Nancy now. He slapped his reins and drove away from Running Fox and his warriors.

As Joe drove off he could not help but have the last say in the matter.

"Indian giver!" he shouted over his shoulder at Running Fox, for having given, then taken away, the plush pelts.

Running Fox only smiled.

Chapter 4

Four Weeks Later
Moon of Berries Ripening—May

The full moon was a huge, bright light in the sky, casting enough of a glow to see by as Running Fox moved stealthily through the dark. His heart was filled with vengeance, for he had heard only one sleep ago that Whiskey Joe had not heeded Running Fox's warnings. He was still peddling his whiskey among the Lakota and Chippewa.

Running Fox had been disappointed to hear his scout's report, that Whiskey Joe had been seen entering and leaving more than one village. He had not been smiling, though, which had to mean that the elders of those villages had sent him away, only for him to secretly meet later with the young braves away from the eyes of their chiefs and elders. After this he had a large smile on his face.

The scout had watched Whiskey Joe ride away, and then he had seen how those young braves had gone and sat by a stream with their jugs of spirit water, laughing and drinking.

He had not stayed to see anything further of their behavior. He had seen it before, how the young braves would become loud and boisterous, then after drinking for so long, would pass out.

The effect this spirit water was having on these youths' brains was startling to consider. Surely it was warping them, making the youths who would one day be warriors unable to function as a powerful warrior must in order to keep his family safe and fed.

Because of all those things, plus being so angry at Whiskey Joe over having ignored Running Fox's latest threat, Running Fox was now climbing through a window and standing over the bed of a woman who would play the main role in his vengeance against the whiskey peddler, for Running Fox knew what she meant to the evil man.

Did not all fathers adore their daughters? And would not all fathers put their daughters' safety even before their own if given that choice?

It did puzzle Running Fox, though, why this man would include his daughter in the evil of his whiskey sales. Was this father too blinded by the expensive pelts he got from the red man and the gold coins he got from the white man to realize the evil he did against his own daughter by including her in his business of whiskey trading?

As the moon spilled through the window onto the sleeping form of the white man's daughter, revealing again to Running Fox just how beautiful she was, it made him almost turn around and leave.

He was torn about what he had planned to do—take the woman in order to get back at a man who could not be made to see reason.

Surely if the man found his daughter missing, it would make him think twice when he started to leave on any more whiskey runs.

He would surely see his daughter's lovely face in his mind's eye and remember that her fate now lay in his own hands, not actually in the abductor's, for if the whiskey peddler proved that he would no longer deal in whiskey among the Indian community, but instead would sell it only to the whites, his daughter would be returned to him safe and unharmed.

Or should Running Fox leave and try to find another way to get his point across to the white man?

He remembered all the times he had dealt, eye to eye, with the whiskey man, trying so hard to make him see reason. Running Fox knew that nothing he had said or done thus far had achieved his goal.

Ay-uh, yes, he must go forward with his plan.

Nothing else had moved the evil man's heart.

Surely the absence of his daughter would.

With a determination in his dark eyes, Running Fox yanked his knife from the sheath at his right side.

Dressed in only a breechclout and moccasins tonight, his long black hair held back from his face by a beaded headband, he leaned over the woman whose name he knew was Nancy and clasped his free hand over her mouth.

When her eyes flew open, he saw fear locked in them.

He hated causing such fear, for that was the last thing he wanted to achieve.

But as he had devised this plan, he had considered all aspects of it and knew she would be afraid at first but would soon know she was in no danger.

Harming her was not in the plan.

"I am not here to frighten you," he said, just loud enough for her to hear. He had studied this house more than once and had watched the lamps lighted in the rooms and then had seen who was in which room.

He had discovered that her *ahte*'s, father's, and mother's rooms were far from where he had seen Nancy going each night and lighting her lamp.

He knew that he did not have to concern himself with her parents awakening—unless she screamed.

And he would make certain she had no reason

to, once he convinced her that he meant her no true harm.

Nancy was petrified. She couldn't see the intruder clearly without her eyeglasses, but she recognized the voice.

She so badly wanted to believe that Chief Running Fox wouldn't harm her, and something deep inside her told her that he wouldn't.

Even when Running Fox had been giving her stepfather strict warnings, there had still been something warm and kind in the young chief's voice.

Trying hard to be brave and to make herself truly believe that this man wouldn't harm her, Nancy nodded her head in an effort to let him know that she felt safe enough in his presence.

He saw her nodding and took that to mean that she wouldn't scream were he to move his hand, that for now she had accepted her fate.

But he felt she needed more convincing before he took his hand from her mouth.

"Do not make any noise," he said. He showed her the knife. "The knife is a quick silencer."

Nancy's heart skipped several beats as she only now realized the true threat.

He had a knife!

She hadn't been able to see it without her eyeglasses.

Would he truly use it on her if she didn't cooperate?

Had she been wrong about this Indian?

Was he evil, through and through?

Was his plan to take her, then defile or murder her?

After Chief Running Fox had warned Joe not to continue his whiskey peddling among the Indians, Joe had ignored him.

She had known at the time that Chief Running Fox would retaliate in some way.

Never would she have guessed that she would be his choice for achieving vengeance against her stepfather.

"I will remove my hand, but again, I warn you not to scream or cry out," Running Fox said softly.

She nodded.

Slowly he slid his hand aside.

He watched as she took several deep breaths, then seemed to be reaching for something on the table beside her bed.

If it was a firearm, she was not as intelligent as he'd hoped she would be.

She surely knew the quickness of a knife, although he knew he could never use it on her. The more he was with her, the more he saw so much about her that caused his heart to race, a reaction unlike any woman before her had caused.

"What are you wanting?" he asked, seeing how she as quickly drew her hand back.

"My eyeglasses," she murmured. "I can't see without them."

"Eyeglasses?" Running Fox said, his eyebrows forking.

Realizing that he surely had no idea what she was talking about, and desperately needing the eyeglasses if he was there to abduct her, which seemed to be the only thing that made sense, she explained to him what they were and how she was almost blind without them.

Surprising to her, he plucked them from the table and handed them to her.

Her fingers trembled as she put them on. Then she saw him—truly saw him—for the first time.

Everything within her seemed to be melting when she saw his noble handsomeness.

His face was sculpted.

His eyes were as dark as all midnights, and he seemed to be as taken by her as she was by him.

And since he was wearing only a breechclout, she saw just how muscled he was.

But feeling unnerved by how scarcely he was clothed, Nancy jerked her eyes up again and gazed into eyes that mesmerized her.

His utter handsomeness truly matched his voice, as she had known it would!

"You can see now?" Running Fox asked, search-

ing her eyes through the glass, mystified by someone having to wear such strange things in order
to see.

"Yes," Nancy murmured.

Then she blurted out, "Why are you here? Why
are you doing this? It's because of my stepfather,
isn't it?"

"*Ay-uh*, yes," Running Fox said. "It is because of
a broken promise. Your father's."

"I thought so," she said, knowing how blatantly
Joe had broken those promises, time and again.
"What are your plans for me?"

"I will take you with me," Running Fox said.
"Your absence should make your father realize the
true wrong in those broken promises."

"But—" Nancy started to argue but was interrupted by Running Fox.

"*Hakamya-upo*, come. You must come with me,"
Running Fox said. "But I will allow you to take a
dress of your liking, a warm cloak, and shoes. It is
a Moon of Berries night. Those nights can be cold."

"I know," Nancy said, in awe of a man who
would truly think of her welfare and at the same
time be abducting her. "Can I take the time to
change here from my gown into a dress before we
leave?"

He was impressed that she had lost her fear and
was ready to do as he required of her without further discussion.

She seemed to understand.

He hoped so, for he did not want to think that she was pretending not to be afraid while in her heart she was.

"*Ay-uh*, yes," he said, stepping away from her. "I shall turn my back long enough for you to change." He leaned his face into hers. "Do not betray my trust as your father has betrayed me with lies."

"Stepfather," she said, correcting him. "He is not my true father."

"Step . . . father . . . ?" Running Fox said, forking his eyebrows. "I do not know of such a thing as a stepfather."

"You are fortunate," she murmured.

He turned his back.

She glanced toward the door, her pulse racing, then at him and how trustingly he had turned his back so that she could change into a dress.

She chose not to betray that trust. She hurriedly changed.

She knew she wouldn't get far even if she tried to escape. And she most certainly wouldn't alert Joe to what was happening. She understood why the young chief was doing this, and she wouldn't want to jeopardize his plans. She truly didn't believe that he would harm her in any way.

"What is a stepfather?" Running Fox asked, breaking the silence, yet not loud enough for anyone but her to hear.

She explained how her true father had died, and how her mother had been awed by Joseph Brock's fancy words and money. She even told him that she had retained her father's last name—Partain.

She explained to Running Fox that her mother had not realized what sort of life Joseph Brock would force on her and her daughter.

"And so you care little for the man?" Running Fox asked, as Nancy stepped around in front of him, all dressed, a fur-trimmed cloak around her shoulders.

"I care nothing for him," Nancy said dryly.

"Leaving is then not all that troublesome to you?" Running Fox asked, searching her eyes through the glass of her eyeglasses.

"I am concerned only about the worry this will cause my mother," Nancy murmured, not fearing to be truthful with him. If he only knew, he was actually doing her a favor. She had been trying to devise a way of escape.

She no longer had to.

"Come," Running Fox said, sliding his knife back inside its sheath.

He placed his hands at Nancy's waist and lifted her through the window, then hurried out himself.

He looked to each side, then ahead.

When he saw no one who could be a threat, he took Nancy's hand and led her quickly into the deep shadows of the trees.

The moon's glow revealed to Nancy two horses that were tied to a low limb.

"You ride one and I the other," Running Fox said, starting to lift her into the saddle of the coal-black stallion. He stopped when he felt her tightening up.

"I don't know how to ride a horse," Nancy said, swallowing hard, causing his hands to drop away from her.

"You do not know how to ride?" he said, his eyes widening in wonder. "All women should know the skill of riding."

"My true father did not see the need, and my stepfather never took the time to teach me," she explained.

She didn't want to share with him something else—that she had no idea how to fire a gun either.

She understood why her true father hadn't taught her. He was always there to defend her—until the day he died so unexpectedly.

"You will ride with me," Running Fox said and lifted her onto his steed.

He tied the other horse's reins into his and then mounted in front of Nancy.

As though it was a natural thing to do, as though she had done this many times before, Nancy swept her arms around Running Fox's waist as he rode off with her.

After they were far away from Dry Gulch, he

looked over his shoulder at her. "I am mystified by someone having to wear such strange magnifying things in order to see," he blurted. "Surely your eyes need medicine. When we arrive at my village, I will call my people's shaman to my lodge and he will make your eyes well."

"How can a shaman know what to do about my problem, to make me see without my eyeglasses, when all of the white doctors I have ever gone to haven't been able to? Doc Harris, especially, is knowledgeable of such things and he tried everything," Nancy said, not wanting to hope that the shaman might truly know how to help her.

Surely she was doomed to wear the hideous things for the rest of her life.

"The oil of the deer's leg is a medicine for wounds of the eyes," Running Fox said. "Once my shaman anoints your eyes with this ointment, you will no longer need the strange things you wear on your nose."

"Thank you for your thoughtfulness, but I truly doubt that your shaman, or anyone else, will ever be able to help me see again without my eyeglasses," Nancy said. She was disappointed, but then she felt gratitude that Running Fox did seem to care enough to want to help her. Yet he still was taking her captive.

She said nothing else to him, just waited to see what his next move would be. She hoped that she had not been wrong to see the good in this chief, rather than the bad.

Suddenly Nancy swallowed hard and her eyes widened when she saw a village of tepees up ahead, fires inside the lodges sending a soft glow of orange through their buckskin coverings.

Everyone seemed to have retired for the night.

Nancy stiffened when Running Fox stopped behind a larger tepee. She assumed that it was his. She was in awe of the many horses in a corral a few feet from the tepee, all of them beautiful.

Running Fox said nothing as he drew a tight rein, dismounted, then lifted her from the saddle.

She stood back and watched him place his steed among the others. Then he turned to her, his dark eyes imploring her.

"We have farther to go, but not on a horse," he explained.

"How . . . then . . . ?" Nancy asked, her eyes wide.

"Canoe," he said, taking her hand and leading her down to the river.

"Where are we going?" Nancy asked as he lifted her into one of the many canoes that were beached there.

"You will soon see" was all that Running Fox said.

He climbed into the birch-bark canoe and was

soon paddling his way across the dark water, away from the village.

Nancy hugged herself, a shiver racing across her flesh as she tried to see ahead of her, where he seemed intent on taking her.

The moon was now covered by clouds.

Nancy had no idea where he was going, or why!

She was only now becoming afraid of what his true intentions might be for her.

She felt like a fool for having helped make this so easy for him!

She turned and looked over her shoulder.

She could no longer see the tepees behind her.

All she could see was swirls of fog that seemed suddenly there, closing in on her and Running Fox.

Chapter 5

When it finally occurred to Nancy where they might be headed—Ghost Island—panic and terrible fear gripped her insides. She had heard about this island but had never actually seen it. It was far from shore, only a blur when anyone tried to see it. Most of the time it was shrouded with some strange kind of fog, making it mystical and frightening for those who knew about its existence.

Ghost Island was known to be the burial ground of the Fox Band of Lakota, which she knew was Running Fox's band.

Traveling through fog now in the canoe, her fingers tightly gripping the sides of the birch-bark vessel, she tried to peer through the fog, but saw nothing except its white, strange swirls, which seemed to engulf her, Running Fox, and the canoe.

She no longer felt as safe with Running Fox as she had earlier. She had seen him as a knight in shining armor who had taken her from a life she had abhorred, a rescuer who she truly believed would not harm her. She even believed he would release her when he had achieved his goal.

But now she couldn't stop trembling as the damp sprays of the foggy mist splashed against her face.

She could barely see Running Fox sitting in front of her, rhythmically drawing his paddle through the water.

She looked behind her and saw nothing except that damnable fog.

She was not certain how far back land was now.

Swallowing hard, Nancy said, "Running Fox, please don't take me to that terrible island. I know that's where you are taking me. I—just—don't know why—unless it is to leave me there after perhaps—"

Running Fox looked over his shoulder, trying to see her through the fog but glimpsing only a slight shadow of her. "I did not tell you a falsehood when I told you that I would not harm you," he said. "And my people's island is not a terrible place. It is a place where my people find peace."

"Yes—a final peace, for that's where your people are buried," Nancy cried.

She reached out to try and touch him, but felt only the dampness of the fog.

She lowered her hand to her lap. "I beg of you to reconsider," she said, tears spilling from her eyes. "Please turn around. Don't take me to that island. If you don't take me there, I will cooperate with you, do whatever you ask of me, without any arguments."

Running Fox felt a deep sympathy for her, for he could hear the true fear in her voice as she pleaded with him.

But he would not change his plans.

Not now.

He had begun this act of vengeance.

He would finish it.

He did hate frightening the woman, but soon she would see that her fears were not grounded, that he was taking her to a place of sheer beauty and peace.

It would be a place where she would live a sweet sort of life until he decided to return her to her life as a white woman.

Until then, she had no choice but to do as he said.

She would learn quickly the gentleness of his Lakota people and the wonders of this island where his people came not only to bury their loved ones but also to pray and meditate.

He lowered the tip of his paddle into the water to check the depth and discovered that they were close to shore.

He placed the paddle in the bottom of the canoe and leapt over the side.

Wading in knee-high water over tiny pebbles, he pulled the canoe out of the water and beached it on the rocky shore.

"Come from the canoe," Running Fox said.

"Please reconsider?" she pleaded, searching his eyes, glad that she could see him now, the fog having dissipated.

"I have told you that you have nothing to fear," Running Fox said, extending a hand toward her. "Come of your own volition or I will carry you."

Realizing that her words were wasted on him, and tired of pleading, Nancy sighed heavily and climbed from the canoe.

She hugged herself with her arms, as she watched him drag the canoe and hide it behind thick brush.

He then reached for her.

She went to him reluctantly, but his hand was warm in hers as he took it.

She gazed up at him.

Their eyes met and held in the moonlight, and in his gaze she saw nothing evil or threatening.

Again she saw only kindness and warmth.

Oh, surely she didn't have anything to fear.

Time would tell, however. She peered through the darkness and saw a forest of birch, oak, pine, and cedar trees. She smiled at the loveliness of the setting.

The air was sweet with the smell of pine and cedar, but also smoke.

She looked quickly up at Running Fox. "I smell smoke," she blurted.

"It comes from the lodges," he said, seeing the confusion in her eyes at his mention of lodges. "*Ay-uh*, yes, there are homes on the island. Those who keep the island secure have their homes here. And then there is mine."

"You live here, not in the village we left back on shore?" Nancy asked, her eyes widening.

"I have two homes. I keep a dwelling for when I want to come and be on the island away from the troubles of the world. My main lodge is in the village," Running Fox explained. "There are never any interferences from whites on Ghost Island. None have ever set foot on its soil."

He glanced down at her. "Not until now," he said, their eyes meeting and holding. "You are the first white ever to set foot on the sacred island of my Lakota people."

They were interrupted when a warrior came seemingly out of nowhere. He was dressed the same as Running Fox. Although it was a cool, damp night, he wore only a breechclout and moccasins and carried a huge, powerful bow with an arrow notched on the bowstring.

"Welcome, my chief," Gray Raven said as he un-notched his arrow and lowered the bow to his side.

"Welcome, Gray Raven," Running Fox replied. "It is good that you are careful of who walks on the soil of our island."

"It is good that it is my chief," Gray Raven said, smiling at Running Fox, then frowning when he spotted the wide-eyed face of the woman at his side.

"This is my friend Gray Raven," Running Fox said, nodding toward his warrior. "He is one of the warriors, along with his wife, Soft Star, whose temporary residences are on the island. They will leave soon and others will come. My warriors take turns protecting the island of our ancestors."

"I remember your voice, but not your face," Nancy said softly.

"But you have been close enough to see my face," Gray Raven said, focusing on the contraption on her nose. He had seen white men wearing such contraptions but knew not the reason.

Running Fox saw Gray Raven studying what he now knew was called eyeglasses.

He quickly explained to his friend what they were, and why Nancy was wearing them.

Then Running Fox led Nancy away while Gray Raven returned to his post.

"You will know Gray Raven's wife," Running

Fox said, as they came to a small clearing, where Nancy saw four tepees.

As they walked toward the largest tepee she gazed again at the others, seeing the glow of fire within them, smoke spiraling slowly from the smoke holes at the top of the tepees.

"This is my lodge," Running Fox said, indicating the largest tepee.

Nancy had read that tepees were constructed of as many as eight dressed buckskins, sometimes more, sewed together with sinews.

These tepees were conical in shape.

Running Fox's tepee seemed to be at least twelve feet in height, while the others on the island were less.

As they stepped inside, she noted that surely his was twelve feet in diameter at the bottom and that a fire was burning in a fire pit at the center.

She saw a clean, comfortable setting of mats, skins, and blankets. She also saw various weapons, among them a long lance with feathers attached to one end, quivers of arrows, more than one huge bow, and several firearms, all of which rested against the back of the tepee opposite the entranceway with its buckskin flap.

She noted a huge pot that hung from a spit over the flames of the fire. A delicious aroma wafting from the pot made her hungry.

She blushed and glanced quickly at Running Fox

when the tantalizing scent of the venison stew made her stomach growl.

"Sit," he said, and he led her toward plush pelts that were laid out before the fire.

He removed her cloak and laid it aside, then helped her down onto the pelts.

Surprising her, he reached for a robe with the hair worn on the inside and gently placed it around her shoulders.

"I saw you trembling earlier," he explained. "I am certain you got chilled while in the canoe. This robe will give you warmth, as will the food that I will serve you."

She was more in awe by the minute of this kind, gentle man, whom she knew most women would be terrified of. But the longer she was with him, the less afraid she was.

She could not help but be impressed by Running Fox as she gazed at him at length now, admiring his dignified manner.

"Thank you," Nancy could not help but say when he gave her not only a bowl of food but also a wooden spoon with which to eat it.

As he sat down beside her and began eating the stew, she noticed how his hair was so exuberantly glossy black, worn loose across his shoulders and long down his back.

Seeing him that first time in the breechclout had

made her blush, for it revealed so much of him to her, especially his muscled, splendid physique.

She could not help but be mesmerized by his handsomeness. Had she been able to see him those times she had accompanied her stepfather on the whiskey runs, she would have surely fallen in love with him, although such feelings for an Indian were forbidden, even taboo, in the white community.

As now, sitting so close beside him, so close she could actually smell the cleanliness of his hair and skin, she could hardly help but want to keep glancing at him, her heart throbbing hard inside her chest.

She knew no fear of him, but she did fear the unknown. She wanted to know his plans for her and whether or not he truly meant to ever let her go.

"Why did you bring me to the island instead of to your main village?" Nancy blurted out as she rested her spoon in the empty bowl.

He looked into her eyes. "Why?" he repeated softly. "You are here because no white man will look for you while you are on Ghost Island."

He stood and took the soiled dishes, set them outside, then went back into the tepee and sat beside Nancy.

"There are only three warriors and their families who live here on our island," he said. "They are here to protect the island. Each new moon brings three new families to live here so that all families can eventually share in the responsibilities of guarding the graves of loved ones who have passed on before them."

"This island is where all of your people are buried once they die?" Nancy asked, truly curious.

"Since so long ago, *ay-uh*, yes, my ancestors, and my people's ancestors, were buried here," Running Fox said. "My own parents are among those who safely rest in their graves here for eternity."

"I'm sorry you had to experience such losses," Nancy said, truly sorry, for she would never forget the pain of losing her beloved father, and even a tiny sister who had lived only a few months.

"They are gone, yet they are always with me," Running Fox said, patting his chest over his heart. "They are here, always, in my heart. I am never without them or the love they gave me before illnesses took them away from me."

"I also feel my father with me," Nancy said, a sob catching in her throat. "My true father was a man so different from my stepfather. He would have never forced such a life on me. Not only does my stepfather make me accompany him on whiskey runs, he makes me sing in his Crystal Palace at Dry Gulch."

"I know of that place," Running Fox said bitterly. He forked an eyebrow. "It is evil. And you were made to sing there?"

Nancy nodded and lowered her eyes. "I hated it so," she said softly, then looked up at Running Fox. She smiled. "I won't be performing there tomorrow, though. I will not be there for him to force this upon me."

Running Fox saw how she smiled about not having to go to that place and knew that without even knowing it, he had helped this woman.

The guilt of having to use her to achieve his vengeance no longer lay as heavy on his heart, for her smile as she spoke of how she had been forced to perform told him much about her that made his heart light.

She was a good woman forced to do bad things by an evil man who claimed her as his daughter.

"It is good to see you smile, for it was with a heavy heart that I chose to include you in the vengeance I have planned against Whiskey Joe," Running Fox said, as he shoved a log into the fire, causing flames to dance around it.

He sat back, his eyes holding hers. "What I have done is to find the best way to make the whiskey peddler pay for not having heeded my warnings," he said. "It was apparent that you were important to him, for the whiskey man referred to you as his daughter."

"And I always cringed when he referred to me as his daughter. In truth, I detest that man and what he does," Nancy said, hoping that admitting so much to this chief wouldn't be dangerous.

In all actuality, surely Running Fox did see that he had done her a favor by having taken her from a life she detested.

But there was her mother.

She knew that her mother would be worried sick over her.

"How long do you plan to keep me on the island?" she asked.

"It is my plan to keep you for a while, to make the man suffer and think he has lost you forever. Then I will release you, but only if you promise not to say who took you when I do let you go back to your white world," Running Fox said, hoping he was not telling her too much of the plan. Thus far she did seem to be the sort he could be open with.

"You would truly trust that I wouldn't tell?" Nancy asked, her eyes wide.

"You would have to offer an explanation to those whites who ask, especially your mother, but all that you would have to say was that it was Indians who abducted you, and not mention which ones," Running Fox said. "There are many Indians in this area who have warned Whiskey Joe about peddling his whiskey, yet he still chances it. The whiskey man cannot go up against all Indians in order to find you, should he attempt to."

"But why abduct me only to release me?" Nancy asked guardedly.

"You will tell him that your abduction and release is only a warning this time," Running Fox said. "If Whiskey Joe continues to peddle his whiskey among our Lakota, and even the Chippewa, the next time it will be he who is taken from his bed in the middle of the night, not the one he calls his daughter."

Running Fox sighed heavily and looked into her eyes again. "I do not enjoy abducting a lovely white woman such as you, but I had no choice. Nothing else I did made Whiskey Joe take notice," he said. "And I know that when I do release you, you will not bring trouble into my community. I see too much kindness in your behavior toward me. I can tell that you truly understand why you have been abducted. I can tell that you realize the wrong your stepfather is doing."

Nancy cringed at the thought of what might eventually happen to her stepfather. Yet she knew he deserved whatever happened to him, because he was evil through and through.

But mainly she hated the thought of having to go back to a place where she hated to be.

Suddenly she yawned and realized just how sleepy she was.

"Where will you sleep?" she asked.

"I will sleep in the tepee with you," Running Fox said matter-of-factly.

"With . . . me . . . ?" Nancy gulped out, her eyes wide.

"Not exactly, but close," Running Fox said, seeing how she had misinterpreted his plans for their sleeping arrangements. He pointed to a blanket that he had hung for her privacy before he went for her. "You will sleep behind the blanket.

"Do you wish to go to your bed of blankets now?" he asked, rising. "Have you eaten all you want?"

"Yes, to both questions," Nancy said, hoping that she was right to believe and trust him regarding the sleeping arrangements.

He took her gently by an elbow and led her behind the blanket. "This is your bed," he said, nodding toward a thick pallet of furs and blankets. "*Ah-boo*, sleep."

Nancy eyed the blankets, then him, then trustingly sat down on the bed until he stepped away.

Truly tired, she stretched out on the plush bed, listening as Running Fox went to his own.

As the fire's glow lessened, Nancy was still awake. Although she was bone-tired, too much had happened for her to relax enough to sleep.

With her spectacles still on, she peered upward through the smoke hole above and gazed into the starry sky.

She knew that tonight was truly the beginning of the rest of her life, for although she was a captive of one man, she had been freed of another.

It was strange how she felt no fear at all with Running Fox. Instead, he made her feel strangely giddy, and her heart warmed at the mere nearness of him!

Chapter 6

"Oh, Lord! Joe!"

His wife shrieking his name woke Joe quickly.

He hurried into a robe, slid his feet into house slippers, and ran into the corridor just as Carole stepped from Nancy's bedroom.

He stiffened, and a cold panic seized his heart when he saw Carole so pale, with a look of desperation in her eyes. "What is it?" he asked. He hurried to her and gripped her by her shoulders. "What's happened?"

"She—she—she's gone," Carole stammered, her eyes wide with alarm. "My Nancy is gone."

"What do you mean—gone?" Joe asked.

"Her bed has been slept in, but she's not there, and I've looked all through the house and there are no signs of her anywhere," Carole said, a sob catching in her throat. "Joe, I think she's run away."

She stifled a sob behind a hand, then loosened herself from her husband's grip and hurried back into Nancy's room.

"She was so unhappy, Joe," Carole said, tears streaming from her eyes. "I should've paid more attention to that unhappiness. She hated what you forced her to do—all of it."

She ran to Joe and began pummeling against his chest with her fists. "You're at fault," she cried. "You forced too much on her. You—are—at fault!"

He grabbed her by her wrists. "Just shut up," he shouted. "I don't want to hear such talk as that."

He dropped her hands and went into Nancy's room.

He looked slowly around him, his gaze stopping at the open window.

He hurried to it and leaned his head out, counting the horses in the corral. None of them were missing.

"There's one dress missing from her chifforobe of clothes, and her fur-trimmed cloak," Carole said. "One pair of her shoes is also missing."

She went to the end table beside the bed. "As are her eyeglasses," she sobbed out.

She turned to Joe, her jaw tight. "If anything happens to my baby, you're at fault," she shouted. "You, Joe. You!"

"Maybe not," Joe said, kneading his chin as he looked from the bed to the window, then back at the bed. "Perhaps someone abducted her."

Carole stumbled to a plush overstuffed chair and buried her face in her hands. "My baby. My baby."

Joe went to her, grabbed her hand, and yanked her to her feet. He leaned his face into hers. "I was wrong! There was no abduction," he said, his eyes narrowing angrily. "No one would come and take her and wait for her to get dressed, even allow her to get her eyeglasses. That damn Naughty Nancy left on her own, and as far as I'm concerned, good riddance of bad rubbish. I'm bone-tired of her whining."

"Joe!" Carole gasped, then winced when his hold on her wrist tightened. "Please let go. Please?"

He released her, then sank down into a chair himself.

He stared at the floor as he began planning what his next move must be.

"Yeah, I knew for some time just how unhappy she was," he mumbled.

Then he looked up at Carole. She still stood there, as though frozen to the floor, gazing at the empty bed. "Well, all that I can say is that I am better off without one more mouth to feed, anyway," he grumbled, rising from the chair.

He went to Carole and slowly circled her, his eyes assessing her. She was wearing a flimsy

nightgown, and he could see her well-shaped figure beneath it.

She was nothing like some women her age. She
didn't look at all old enough to have a daughter
Nancy's age. She still had a voluptuous figure, and
a pretty oval face and large green eyes.

And she could sing as well as Nancy.

Yes, she could take over all of Nancy's duties,
and he'd make certain she pleased everyone—or
else.

"You can sing for the gents in my establishment,
and you can accompany me on my whiskey runs,"
he said, causing Carole to take a quick, unsteady
step away from him, her face ashen.

"No," she said, clutching her throat. The thought
of doing those things made her feel suddenly nauseous.

She soon broke down again. All she could think
about was Nancy, who didn't even know how to
ride a horse or fire a gun.

Out there all alone and helpless, Carole thought.

But what gave her some comfort was that at least
Nancy was free of her stepfather.

She would try to think on the positive side. Her
daughter was better off, and surely she would find
someone who would sympathize with her plight
and take her in and care for her.

Still crying, Carole wiped at her eyes, and was

startled when Joe shouted at her and gave her a shove that almost sent her to the floor.

"Stop that bawling!" he shouted. He grabbed Carole and yanked her close. He glared into her eyes. "Pretty wife, you've things to do besides cry and waste your time worrying about your worthless daughter."

"One day you'll get yours," Carole said, hating the man she had fallen for too quickly after her husband had died.

Of late, after seeing so much of Joe's cruel, evil side, she had begun to wonder if he might even have been involved in her husband's death.

"What are you thinking so hard on?" Joe asked. He placed a finger beneath Carole's chin and lifted it so that he could look directly into her eyes. "Huh? What's on your mind that made you get so quiet?"

"Why, *you*, darling," Carole said in a mocking tone. *"You."*

"I don't think I want to hear what you were thinking about me, for if you'd seen that look on your face, you'd have even scared yourself," Joe said.

He stepped away from Carole.

He nodded toward the door. "Go and get dressed and get me some flapjacks on the damn kitchen table," he said flatly. "And be quick about it. You've got a few errands to do today with your husband."

He leaned into her face. "You've some practicing to do on the stage, my sweet," he said. "You've got to get your voice in tune for the gents who'll discover there's someone besides Naughty Nancy to sing for them. Instead, it'll be Naughty Carole."

He circled her for a moment, then stopped and reached for her hair. He ran his fingers slowly through it. "Yep, it's gotta be dyed red," he said dryly. "That's what the gents want. After you get food on the table, dye your hair red."

"No," Carole gasped. She slapped his hand away. She placed her fists on her hips and lifted her chin stubbornly. "I won't, Joe. That's asking too much of me."

"You will, or else," he growled.

He threw his head back in a fit of laughter, then walked on past her and left Nancy's room.

"Oh, Nancy, where are you?" she cried.

"Carole!"

Joe's voice made her flinch. She hurried to her own room and got dressed, then soon found herself dropping pancake dough into hot grease on the stove. She had no choice but to accept her new lot in life. She certainly wasn't brave enough to flee her husband's wrath—a man she now knew was a madman!

"And possibly even a murderer," Carole said to

herself, paling at the thought. If he had gotten enough of her Nancy's complaining, could he have done away with her?

That thought made her tremble.

And she felt trapped. She had no one to turn to, especially not the law in Dry Gulch. Her husband played poker with the sheriff, who was deep in debt to him after losing at cards more than once.

She couldn't even go to the deputies for help. The sheriff and his deputies were best buddies!

She could only pray that Nancy was all right out there somewhere, and that someone had taken pity on her.

She would not allow herself to think that Nancy had been done away with by her husband!

"Where's them flapjacks?" Joe shouted, sauntering into the dining room just as Carole came in with a huge stack of pancakes. "Just look at you. You've got flour all over your face. You'd best change that quick after you dye your hair. We've plenty to please tonight with your singing and looks."

She set the platter of pancakes down on the table, glared at Joe, then hurried to her bedroom and stopped and gazed into the mirror.

She ran her fingers over the wrinkles that had just begun to creep from the corners of her eyes. If they worsened, would Joe tire of her?

Then what would he do to her? she wondered, shivering at the worst she could imagine.

She felt nauseous as she lifted the bottle of dye and opened it. She took one long, last look at her hair before changing it into the hideous red color that she had learned to despise after applying it to Nancy's hair so often.

"He says red hair makes a woman look more passionate," Carole mumbled to herself. She sighed. "He doesn't know what true passion is."

She did. She had had intense passion with her first husband when they made love. She still couldn't believe that she had allowed someone like Joseph Brock to come into her life after being married to such a fine man as her husband Charles.

"But I did, and now I'm paying for it in the worst way," she said, sobbing. "Nancy, oh, Nancy, where are you?"

Chapter 7

It was a strange feeling to wake up somewhere besides her own bed. Especially in a tepee. When Nancy woke with a start as the light poured down onto her face from the smoke hole overhead, she looked immediately at the hanging blanket that hid everything else from her view. Although things were just a blur without her eyeglasses, she immediately remembered where she was. And with whom.

She sat up quickly, her heart pounding, clutching a blanket to her chin and reached for her eyeglasses.

She still sat there, though, unsure of what she should do next. The only sounds she heard were horses just outside the tepee munching on the rich grass, its roots fed by the last winter's snows, now new and thick.

She hadn't expected horses on the island, since it had to be reached by canoe.

Finally Nancy rose from the bed of blankets and pelts and peeked around the blanket that had been hung to give her privacy.

All that she saw was a fire burning in the fire pit and a pot of something cooking over the flames, sending off delicious-smelling aromas.

She could recognize the smell of onions, which she concluded had been gathered wild in the forest, and some sort of meat.

Her meal today, as last night, would be something made from venison.

She looked elsewhere and saw where Running Fox had surely slept. Blankets still held his form within them beside the fire pit. But he was nowhere to be seen.

Again she listened for sounds other than those of the horses.

She still heard nothing, so could only imagine that the women who lived in the three other tepees were either still asleep or already preparing food for their husbands' next meals.

She again gazed at Running Fox's bed, wondering where he might be, then dropped the corner of the blanket back in place and hurried into her clothes.

After running her fingers through her hair, ridding it of the witch's knots and tangles that came while sleeping, she stepped from behind the blanket and tiptoed over to the entrance flap.

Her fingers trembled as she slowly drew the buckskin flap aside and looked around her.

From this vantage point, she saw no movement anywhere, nor did she hear any voices.

This tiny camp sat amid a grove of birch and willow trees.

She looked from tepee to tepee, still seeing no one about, then spotted, a small distance away, what must be the sacred burial ground of Running Fox's ancestors. It was a large piece of land where she could see mounds here and there, which she concluded were the graves.

And then she saw movement.

Breathlessly, she stepped back from the entrance flap, yet still held a corner aside so that she could see who might be there. It was a warrior with a bow slung across his shoulder and a quiver of arrows at his back.

He was walking slowly back and forth, his eyes occasionally glancing guardedly around him.

Nancy concluded that he was the warrior whose duty it was to protect that section of the burial ground. Other guards must be on duty at different locations. She wondered where they might be?

Then she spotted the path that led to the lake and the shore where she knew canoes were beached.

She doubted that anyone had ever come uninvited to this island.

"What must I do?" she whispered, dropping the entrance flap.

She crossed to the fire and knelt beside it, gazing into the flames. While she slept someone had added wood to the fire and someone had come and placed a pot of food over the flames. Had Running Fox done all of this?

Or had one of the women come after having been asked by her chief, so that the white captive would have food?

She was truly hungry. The smell was so tantalizing—yet she had to think of other things now besides eating. Last night, just before she had fallen asleep, something had suddenly come to her that had made her blood run cold.

She had suddenly realized that if she was taken back to live with her stepfather, as Running Fox had said, she would be no better off than before.

She would again be forced to sing in that horrible den of iniquity, and she knew that her stepfather would not heed Running Fox's warnings even after her return.

She knew that he would take his chances in order to gain the Indians' magnificent pelts.

If she was going to have to live that life again, then she must find a way to escape Running Fox now.

She didn't fear Running Fox any longer.

The true fear came from the thought of his returning her to the world that she had been forced into—a world of degradation and shame!

"I must escape," she blurted out, her heart pounding at the thought of what she knew she must do—now, while Running Fox was gone.

"The guards," she whispered, looking quickly at the entrance flap.

Yes, she had to elude the guards.

But how?

There should be three guards to watch out for.

But she knew that they couldn't be everywhere at once.

Wouldn't that give her at least a chance at escaping?

Her pulse racing, Nancy went to the entrance flap and slowly slid it aside.

Again she looked all around outside the tepee.

She saw nothing of the women, and now she didn't even see the one guard that she had seen earlier.

He had gone elsewhere to watch for interlopers.

"And me?" she whispered, thinking that surely the warriors had been instructed to watch out for her trying to escape.

But nothing mattered now.

She was determined to find a new life even though she could not deny having strange feelings for Running Fox.

In truth, she feared those feelings, which she felt must come with infatuation.

No man had ever affected her in such a way, and Running Fox was not just any man. He was an Indian!

Knowing she must leave now, or possibly never have a chance again, Nancy crept outside.

She looked cautiously from side to side.

Then she made a quick dash to the back of the tepee, cringing when her presence made several of the lovely horses whinny.

She was thankful when they quickly returned to munching on the grass, too hungry, it seemed, to worry about the likes of her being near them.

Sighing with relief, she cautiously circled the corral and made her way toward the trees behind the circle of tepees.

She reached the trees and broke into a run, hoping the lake wouldn't be much farther ahead.

All of a sudden, Nancy found herself in a wild plum thicket, the fruit ripe and sweet.

Wasps were buzzing over the rotting fruit that had fallen on the ground.

As several started stinging Nancy, she screamed and fought to get them away from her.

Suddenly through her haze of tears she spotted Running Fox in the distance.

Forgetting why she was there in the first place and so wanting to be freed from the wasps, Nancy cried out to Running Fox. "Please help me," she sobbed, still swatting around her. "I've been stung! They hurt so badly!"

Running Fox had heard Nancy's screams, and he immediately tried to find her. After finding the tepee empty, he'd begun to scour the area, looking for her. Finally, he had seen her through a break in the trees. She had gotten trapped beneath a plum tree, her feet unable to take her from the slippery rotten fruit beneath it.

He saw why she was screaming when he got close enough.

Wasps were everywhere, attacking her.

He could already see several welts on her face and neck, and especially her hands as she continued to swat at them.

When he finally reached her, he ignored the wasps, stepped beneath the tree, pulled Nancy into his arms, and carried her to safety.

"Thank you. Oh, Lord, thank you," Nancy sobbed, clinging to his neck as he ran back in the direction of his small camp.

It seemed that she was on fire everywhere that had been stung by the wasps.

Her face!

Her neck!

Her hands!

One had even managed to get up the sleeve of her dress and attack her there.

Running Fox ran toward the tepee clearing. He said nothing, for he was too full of wonder about why she had been that far from his tepee to think of much else.

There had to be only one answer.

She had decided to try and escape and had gotten trapped by the wasps before she got to the lake.

He gazed down at her, pitying how she must be hurting. For now, he would put the why of everything out of his mind.

The most important thing was to get her to his lodge and send for his shaman so that her stings could quickly be medicated.

When he stepped into the clearing, he saw that the screams had brought the women from their lodges and the men from their posts, their bowstrings notched with arrows.

When they all saw their chief carrying the white woman whose face was marred by red, swollen bites, the warriors lowered their weapons and stared.

"White Owl, go to our village and get our shaman," Running Fox shouted at the oldest warrior.

Running Fox stopped before his tepee. "Go. Hurry. Bring Medicine Bear back to my lodge. Tell him what sort of bites he will be medicating."

"*Hai*, what sort are they?" White Owl asked, handing his bow and quiver to his wife, Moon Shadow.

"Wasp," Running Fox said, then took Nancy inside his lodge and gently laid her on his bed of blankets and pelts.

"I'm hurting so much," Nancy sobbed, her face burning like fire. She gazed into Running Fox's eyes. "How bad are they?"

"There are many, but my shaman will know what to do to take away the fire and the swelling," Running Fox said. He went to the back of his tepee and got a parfleche bag, then laid it beside Nancy. "I have something that might help until Medicine Bear arrives."

Nancy watched him take what looked like herbs from his bag, then combine them with water in a small pot on the fire.

She trembled with pain and waited and watched, knowing that soon the questions would come as to why she had not been in his lodge where he had left her.

She now understood the foolishness of what she had tried, being so unknowledgeable about so many things of the forest. There were many sorts of dangers awaiting someone like her. She knew now that her place was with Running Fox until he finally set her free.

Even then she would not be eager to go, especially if he returned her to her stepfather and the horrors of the life she had while with him.

"What I will apply to your wounds should help," Running Fox said, taking the pot from the fire. It wasn't smoking, which had to mean that it was only warm to the touch, not hot.

Nancy winced as he gently applied the medicine, but was grateful that the mixture took some of the sting from her bites.

She was stunned that he had not yet asked her what she had been doing that far from his tepee.

Of course, she knew that he had guessed. Why else would she be that close to the lake?

She was relieved when he didn't ask her, but instead sat on the other side of the fire from her, his eyes never leaving her.

She gazed shyly at him. "Thank you," she murmured. "You continue to be so kind to me." She lowered her eyes, then gazed over at him again. "I don't deserve your kindness, you know."

He still said nothing, only continued to look at her through the flames of the fire. He wore only a breechclout and moccasins, and she could see more than one place where he also had been stung. He seemed unaware of it—otherwise he would surely have medicated his own stings.

Unnerved by his silence, and so relieved that she wasn't in as much pain, Nancy turned her eyes away from Running Fox.

She stretched out on her side and gazed into the fire as she waited with him for the shaman.

A part of her dreaded someone like the shaman putting his strange sort of medicine on her flesh.

She had always thought shamans and medicine men were something akin to someone who practiced voodoo on people.

She would soon see whether or not that was true.

Suddenly Medicine Bear came into the tepee.

Nancy sat up, in awe of him.

He was a bent old man in a long robe, with snow-white hair that hung to the floor, a man who had carried on his back a large pack as he had entered the dwelling.

Running Fox stood up and greeted Medicine Bear, then gestured toward Nancy. "The woman has many wasp stings," he said.

Medicine Bear turned and gazed down at Nancy, his eyebrows forking when he saw that she wore eyeglasses. He knew of such things. He had seen them on whites before and knew the magic they carried.

He bent down to his knees before her. "Do not be afraid of my medicine," he said kindly. "Mine is the power of medicine and the protector of my people's faith. I ask that you, too, have faith in how I am to medicate you."

"I do," Nancy murmured, feeling Running Fox's eyes on her and knowing that she was expected to show faith in his shaman.

Then she gazed at Medicine Bear again. "Oh, please do help the burn leave the stings," she begged.

"What Running Fox placed there was much too short-lived."

It did not take long for Medicine Bear to apply his own medicinal herbs to Nancy's stings. Then he went to his chief and medicated his.

Medicine Bear looked from his chief to Nancy and then to his chief again. "Soon all signs of the stings will be gone," he said, closing his bag and returning it to his back.

"Thank you so much," Nancy murmured, already feeling at peace, for the burn was all but gone.

Even the welts seemed smaller after the medicine had been applied there, as did Running Fox's seem to have all but disappeared.

"White Owl will return you to your home," Running Fox said, placing a gentle arm around the old man's shoulders and leading him outside.

Nancy breathlessly awaited Running Fox's return, for she knew that soon he would want to know what had taken her from his lodge.

When he did come back inside, he wasn't alone. A lovely Lakota woman who seemed to be Nancy's mother's age came in with him, dressed in a beaded garment and carrying a bowl of food and two wooden spoons.

"I have brought plum duff for your dinner," Moon Shadow murmured as she set the bowl on the floor close to Nancy. She smiled at her chief.

"There is enough for two. I have brought two spoons."

Running Fox smiled. "*Hiye-pila-maya*, thank you," he said, then looked quickly over at Nancy when she gasped at what she knew she was to eat. Something made of plums, the very fruit that had caused her to be trapped beneath its tree so that the wasps could attack her.

Moon Shadow seemed to understand. She laughed softly. "White woman, wasps eat only rotten plums," she murmured. "You and my chief eat fresh."

Nancy smiled nervously as Running Fox walked with Moon Shadow from the tepee, then came back in and gazed down at her.

But he still said nothing to her.

He sat down beside her.

He handed her a spoon and took one for himself.

He began eating from the bowl, glancing over at Nancy, who had yet to take a bite.

"Moon Shadow is skilled at cooking," he said. "Eat. You will discover its goodness."

"I'm not sure," Nancy said, shivering. "If not for that plum tree, I—"

She stopped short from saying what she was thinking, realizing that even though she had not said it, Running Fox seemed to know that she was blaming the tree for stopping her escape.

"Will you try to leave again?" he asked.

Nancy was taken off guard by the question. She smiled awkwardly.

Then she said, "No."

He smiled and waited for her to take a bite of the plum duff.

Nancy picked up the spoon and slid a bite cautiously into her mouth.

Her eyes widened. "Why, it's delicious," she said, actually licking the spoon.

She saw an amused glint in Running Fox's eyes, then she smiled almost shyly at him. "I truly thank you for what you did for me today," she murmured. "If you hadn't come, I probably would have died. I'm certain the wasps would have continued stinging me until I passed out."

She wondered if he saw more than gratitude in her eyes.

Could he tell that she was falling in love with him?

Ah, but she was, oh, so in love with him.

The moment he had grabbed her up into his arms today and rescued her from the wasps, she knew that she was lost, heart and soul, to him.

Actually, she had never felt more protected than at that moment when his arms held her close to him as he ran back to his tepee.

"I am sorry that you felt the need to flee my island—and Running Fox," he said, his voice thick with emotion. "I do hope that you do not have that same need again and that you know that while you are here, you have nothing to fear—that I would never allow anything to happen to you."

He saw much in her eyes and smile. He was fighting feelings that he knew were wrong. From the moment he had seen her in so much pain, so harmed by the wasps, he knew that he was lost, heart and soul, to her.

Her smile, the radiance of it, was all that he needed in order to know that she was there for as long as he wished her to be.

Chapter 8

Finally, after four days, the welts on Nancy's face began to clear up, as did those few inflicted on Running Fox.

Nancy and Running Fox had already eaten their morning meal. She tried to ignore his presence, even though the longer she was with him the more in awe of him she became. He was different from any men she had ever known.

As Nancy stroked her long hair with a brush that Running Fox had given to her, one that was made of porcupine quills, she could feel him watching her.

He had said that he was leaving soon to go into council with his warriors at his main village.

Yet he seemed to keep delaying it, and she began to feel self-conscious as he watched her continue to brush her hair.

She could feel the heat of his eyes on her, clean into her heart, making it thud wildly within her chest.

The way he gazed into her eyes made her almost melt, and she knew the dangers in that. Her only reason for being there was to achieve vengeance against her stepfather.

Running Fox had even told her that she would be allowed to leave once his scheme was concluded.

So much inside her heart said that she didn't ever want to leave Running Fox.

Yet she knew the foolishness of thinking that way. He was surely only intrigued by her hair, and perhaps the color of her eyes, which was unlike that of many women's eyes, for the violet color was unique in its own way.

Was he as in awe of her, the person, as he was of other things about her?

"I have never seen such a red color of hair before," he blurted out, so suddenly that Nancy dropped the hairbrush.

"Nor have I ever seen such beautiful eyes," he then said.

Nancy turned and smiled shyly at him as he picked up the hairbrush and handed it back to her.

"Thank you," she murmured, clutching the handle, too unnerved to continue brushing her hair.

He reached out toward her. "May I touch your hair?" he asked softly.

Nancy's face flooded with color. She smiled at Running Fox again, then nodded.

"Yes, if you wish," she murmured, everything within her reacting to his touch as he did run his fingers ever so slowly and gently through her hair.

"It is quite lovely," Running Fox said, then drew his hand quickly away again, as though he had just realized what he was doing.

He stepped toward the entrance flap. "I must leave you now," his words rushed out. "Soft Star or Moon Shadow will come sometime today and sit with you so that you will not be so alone."

"I'm used to being alone," Nancy said softly. "When I was not being made to do things for my stepfather, I stayed in my room."

"What did you do there?" Running Fox asked curiously.

"I read books," Nancy said. She reached up and readjusted her eyeglasses on her nose. "I love to read. It has always been my way to escape the real world, a world that has not been so pleasant for me."

"And now you are a captive," Running Fox said, lifting the entrance flap. "I am sorry to have brought more hardships into your life, but it was necessary. It seemed the one thing that could hurt the whiskey runner's heart the most."

She wanted to tell him that he was wrong, that Joseph had no feelings whatsoever for her.

But something had occurred to her during their conversation about the color of her hair.

She now knew a way to get back at Running Fox for having abducted her.

Although she enjoyed this newfound way of life, where she felt so free, she was uncomfortable with being Running Fox's captive.

And because of that, she wanted to find a way to get back at him without putting herself in danger.

She just wanted to make a statement.

And she would.

Today.

She was free to come and go from the tepee without escort because she had had one bad experience while trying to leave. Running Fox seemed confident that she wouldn't try again.

"I would like to wash my hair," she said, so suddenly that Running Fox dropped the entrance flap.

"You have the freedom to do so," he said.

He nodded to his left. "There is a creek not far from this camp," he said. "The water runs clear. It is where the wives of my warriors who are assigned to the island wash their hair."

He went to his bag of bathing supplies and took out a bar of the soap that his people made for their personal baths. "This is my people's soap," he said, holding it out to Nancy. "It is good for hair washing."

"Thank you," Nancy said. She gazed at the soap, wondering what it might be made from, since so many things of the Lakota were made differently from the way whites made their things.

But it didn't matter. It was soap. She knew that now that she had an actual bar of soap, she would be able to achieve her goal.

She smiled at Running Fox, wondering if he could see the gleam in her eyes through her eyeglasses.

"I must go now," Running Fox said, wondering about a strange look that Nancy suddenly had in her eyes.

But having spent too much time discussing such things as hair, he turned and hurried out of the tepee.

Nancy eyed the soap, then the closed entrance flap. She smiled broadly as she stepped out into the morning air—which, thank goodness, was warm enough for hair washing.

What she was about to do would achieve more than one thing for her. Not only would it make Running Fox wonder why she would do such a thing, but it would also do something that she had wanted to do since the moment her stepfather had handed her the dye and ordered her to place it on her hair.

Her stepfather had more than once told her that men saw red hair as more passionate than the other colors.

"More passionate, pooh," she whispered to herself as she walked away from the tepees and toward the creek that had been pointed out to her.

She felt eyes on her and knew that the women were surely watching her and wondering where she was going after her terrible bout with the wasps.

They might be wondering what sort of trouble would this white women get in this time!

She smiled to herself, knowing that what she was about to do would truly raise the women's eyebrows.

Her pulse raced as she knelt down beside the creek listening to the birds singing above her, on the limbs of the oak trees.

She recognized the song of the robin, as well as the cardinal, which reminded her of long-ago days on her father's farm when she had eagerly awaited the arrival of spring.

Smiling, she lowered her hair into the water, the first sting of its coldness sending shivers up and down her spine.

She wet her hair thoroughly, then soaped it until the suds were bubbling all over her head.

She scrubbed and scrubbed with her fingers until they were almost raw, but she knew that if she wanted to achieve her goal, she had to use a lot of soap and elbow grease.

She rinsed her hair, then soaped it again, rinsed it one last time, lifted it from the water, and wrung it out as best she could.

Her heart throbbed in her chest as she peered into the mirror of the water, a large smile erupting on her face when she saw her reflection.

Her hair was restored to its original rich black color.

She studied her likeness in the water for a moment, noting how tan she was from traveling the countryside with her stepfather.

Why, with her hair color now being the same as the Indian women's, except for her violet eyes and the eyeglasses, she could pass for a Lakota maiden.

She felt immensely proud that she had done something all on her own without any man forcing her.

All for the sake of pleasing the gents who frequent his Crystal Palace, he had said, standing there that day until she poured that first drop of dye from the bottle onto her hair.

He hadn't cared that she cried from having to do it, for she knew that she looked like a hussy with that color of hair.

"Never again," she said aloud, drawing the attention of the women as she returned to the small camp.

A lovely woman who seemed perhaps to be

twenty-five years of age approached Nancy, who stiffened when the woman reached a hand to her hair and touched it, then drew her hand away again.

"Where did the color go?" Soft Star asked, still looking at Nancy's hair. "It is no longer the color of flame."

Nancy held out the bar of soap toward her. "I used this to take it away," she murmured.

"Soap?" Soft Star gasped, stepping away from Nancy. "I use soap, but it does not change the color of my hair."

Nancy laughed softly. "No, it wouldn't. You see, my hair had been dyed the color of red, as I believe you sometimes dye your pelts to give them a different color."

"Why would you do that?" Soft Star asked, again touching Nancy's hair, which was now almost dry. "The color of flame was pretty."

Nancy's smile faded. "I did not like it at all," she said. "It was something forced on me by someone I detest. Otherwise I would have always had hair the same color as yours, which I love."

Soft Star drew her hand away from Nancy's hair, then touched her own. "*Ay-uh*, yes, I prefer my own color, too. Were I to have the color of the sun in my hair, I would not be myself."

"That is exactly how I felt when I was forced to dye my hair," Nancy said, sighing.

"I am called by the name Soft Star," the woman said, lifting her chin proudly. "I am wife to Gray Raven."

"Gray Raven," Nancy said, in her mind's eye remembering him very well. He had been kind to her from the beginning.

In fact no one on this island had made her feel uneasy.

"Yes," she said. "I know him."

Nancy slid the bar of soap into the pocket of her dress, then dared to reach out and touch the beads on Soft Star's dress. "I love the fancy beadwork on your dress." She lowered her hand, then gazed down at the fringed hem. "I also like the softness of your dress and the fringe at the hem."

"My dress today is made of doeskin and it is the softest of all my dresses," Soft Star murmured. "I did the beadwork myself. It is something I enjoy."

"You are very talented," Nancy said. Her eyes widened when instead of replying to the compliment, Soft Star turned and hurried away.

"What did I say wrong?" Nancy wondered to herself, as she returned to Running Fox's tepee.

She began brushing her hair, then stopped and turned toward the entrance flap when Soft Star came inside, a dress hanging across one of her arms and a pair of moccasins in her hand.

Nancy saw that she also held another bundle, but it was too folded up for her to tell what it was.

"These are yours to wear if you want them," Soft Star said, offering the dress and the leggings to Nancy, who hesitated to accept them.

"They are mine to do with as I please," Soft Star quickly said. "I please to give them to you."

Realizing that her hesitation might be taken the wrong way, and not wanting to humiliate the lovely woman, Nancy held her arms out and allowed Soft Star to lay first the dress across them and then the other garment.

Soft Star set the moccasins down close to Nancy's feet.

"You are so generous," Nancy murmured, holding the garments out to get a better look. Then she realized the clothing that she had not immediately recognized was leggings. They were beautifully trimmed with porcupine quills.

"Thank you. Thank you so much."

"I will leave now," Soft Star said. "But it would please me so much if you would wear what I have given to you."

"And I shall," Nancy said, smiling at Soft Star. "Again, thank you. I love it all."

Beaming, Soft Star turned and left the tepee.

Nancy gazed at what she had been given, then eagerly removed her clothes, replacing them with the Indian garments.

She ran her hands across the front of the dress.

She had never felt anything as soft.

And she loved the wonders of the moccasins on her feet!

Wanting to see how she looked, and wondering what Running Fox would think when he saw her transformation, she ran from the tepee and again went to the creek.

She leaned over the water, adjusted her eyeglasses so that she could see better, then sighed with pleasure when she saw just how pretty she did look in the beautiful dress.

But there was one thing missing.

She quickly reached back and braided her hair into one long braid, tying the end with a strand of fringe.

Her pulse racing, she again inspected her reflection.

She seemed totally transformed.

Oh, Lord, how *would* Running Fox feel when he saw her?

Would he think she was mocking the women by trying to look like them?

Or would he be touched by her wanting to look like them?

Suddenly a reflection was in the water next to hers.

Running Fox's!

Blushing, Nancy turned to face him.

Running Fox could not help but stare at the difference in her hair.

How could it be one color, and then another?

"How did you take away the color of your hair and where did you get clothes of my people?" Running Fox asked suspiciously, as he tried to take in the many changes to her appearance.

Then he looked into her eyes and saw that he had made her uneasy by his quick questions.

He reached a hand to her cheek. "I did not mean to alarm you," he said, his voice gentler.

"But how *did* you lose the color of your hair?" Running Fox asked, lowering his hand to his side. "And why did you think that you should?"

Nancy momentarily lowered her eyes. Then she gazed into his.

Deep within her, where her desires were formed, she truly didn't want to disappoint or anger Running Fox.

For the first time in her life, she found herself caring for a man sensually.

She hurriedly explained about her stepfather making her dye her hair and why, and how she had hated it.

She failed to tell him what role Running Fox himself had played in her having decided to change her hair back to its normal color—that she wanted to get back at him for having taken her from her bed in the middle of the night.

"The dress, leggings, and moccasins were given to me by Soft Star," she said softly. "I can give them back if you wish, but there isn't anything I can do now about my hair. I'm almost certain you don't have hair dyes or you would have known why mine could change so easily from one color to another."

She lowered her eyes, then looked into his again. "Are you angry with both me and Soft Star?" she asked.

"No, I am not angry with either of you," Running Fox said. "Intrigued, but not angry."

He held a hand out for her. "*Hakamya-upo*, which in my language says to come," he said. "Soft Star has been asked to bring food to my lodge."

Hugely relieved that he wasn't angry with her or Soft Star, Nancy walked beside him, pride in her step for the first time in years.

She had seen how her transformation had made her pretty, prettier than she had ever been in the lavish clothes that her stepfather had made her wear, and she was glad that Running Fox had seemed to enjoy the change too.

As they walked into the camp, all eyes moved to them, then lingered mainly on her.

Nancy was glad when he took her into the tepee.

"Sit," he said softly, gesturing with a hand toward the blankets spread out beside the fire.

"Did you have a successful council with your warriors?" she asked as she sat down beside the

fire, wanting to find a way to make things comfortable between them again.

"It was a good council," he said, settling down
beside her, then looking up quickly at Soft Star as
she came into the lodge, carrying a wooden platter
of food.

Nancy's eyes and Soft Star's met.

They exchanged smiles, making Nancy feel that
she might have a friend for the first time in her life.

While she was growing up, there were many
miles between her house and those where others
her same age lived, so she had always had to devise
ways of entertaining herself without a friend to
share it with.

Then, when her mother had married her stepfather and moved into Dry Gulch, too much had
been put upon Nancy for her to be able to make any
close, special friends.

But now?

She did feel something special between herself
and Soft Star.

It made a warmth in her heart that she had never
felt before.

Running Fox took the platter of food, then smiled
at Soft Star and nodded toward the entrance flap in
a silent way of thanking her, then excusing her.

Nancy gazed at the variety of food on the platter,
all of which could be eaten with her fingers.

She questioned him with her eyes when he gazed at her.

"The meal today is a simple one," he said, as though he understood her hesitation in taking anything from the platter. "There are small cakes made from berries of all kinds that are gathered by my people's women, then dried in the sun. The dried foods are used in soups, too, and for mixing with the pounded jerked meat and fat to form a much prized delicacy."

He saw her eyes move to the vegetables. "You can eat a strip of teepsinna. It is starchy but solid, with a sweetish taste." He smiled as his eyes dropped to her waist, and then he gazed into her eyes again. "It is also fattening."

"What else is on the platter?" Nancy asked, still hesitant about what to eat and ignoring what he had said about the one vegetable being fattening.

"There is also some wild sweet potato, which is found in the riverbeds, but there is one thing in particular that was brought today that you might be hesitant about eating were I to tell you where they were found before being prepared for eating," Running Fox said, smiling almost amusedly at Nancy.

"Which are they, and why would I hesitate to eat them?" Nancy cautiously asked.

"It is a savory vegetable, a bean," Running Fox said, pointing to a pile of brownish-colored objects.

"The women rob the field mice homes of these beans."

Nancy paled and gasped.

"Tiny mice gather wild beans for their winter use," Running Fox said, smiling slowly at her reaction. "The storehouses for these beans, made by the animals, are under a peculiar mound which the untrained eye is unable to distinguish from an anthill. There are many pockets underneath, into which the animals gather their harvest. Usually in the month that white people call September, a woman comes upon a suspected mound, usually by accident. The heel of her moccasin might cause a place to give way on the mound. She then settles down to rob the poor mice of the fruits of their labor. It is quite a savory vegetable when cooked by the Lakota women."

"The vegetable is actually eaten after—after—having been in the homes of mice?" Nancy choked out, mortified at the thought of taking even one bite of those beans.

"Like I said, it is a savory vegetable loved by all of my people," Running Fox said, plucking up a couple of the baked beans and popping them into his mouth.

Nancy's eyes were wide as she watched him chew the beans.

Then when he took two more from the platter and offered them to her, she visibly shivered. "No, I don't think so," she murmured, then eyed everything else and wondered where it might have been before being turned into the food the Lakota actually ate!

Nancy's stomach growled. She knew that if she didn't eat now, while food was being offered to her, it might be a long time before the next meal.

She held her breath and closed her eyes while she put several of the beans in her mouth.

Then her eyes opened wide and she gazed at Running Fox, stunned at just how delicious those beans were!

Running Fox saw her reaction and only smiled.

She had much to learn, he thought to himself. And she must, for the longer he was with her, the more doubtful he was that he could ever return her to her world, even though he had promised her that he would.

Looking at her now, so beautiful with her hair the same color as that of his people, and wearing the clothes of his people, he was even more infatuated with her than before!

He saw her as a woman he could love, and—perhaps—already did!

Chapter 9

The fire sent off a warm glow, making dancing shadows along the inside walls of the buckskin tepee.

Having gotten through the meal all right, having even enjoyed the beans, although she knew where they had been "harvested," Nancy felt at peace with herself as she watched Running Fox working on a pipe.

It was strange how it seemed so normal to sit there with him as night fell.

It was like those wonderful, peaceful evenings not so long ago when her father was still alive and she sat with her parents beside their fireplace at their country home, relaxing, sometimes talking, sometimes just enjoying being with one another.

Her mother had laid her knitting aside, and her

father, who enjoyed reading more than she had ever thought a man might, laid aside his book.

He, too, had worn glasses, but mainly when he read, and she had always thought that his eye problems had come from straining his eyes as he read by candlelight or firelight in the evenings.

His days were too full to read then, so the nighttime hours were all that were left for him to enjoy. He mainly read mysteries.

Nancy had taken up his love of reading. Sometimes she had read into the wee hours of the night by candlelight after her parents had gone to bed.

But all of that had changed when her mother married Joseph Brock. Nancy was too worn out from the activities forced on her by her stepfather to do anything but fall into bed each night, finding her escape in sleep, not books.

"Is the pipe you are making for some sort of ceremony, or is it for your own enjoyment?" Nancy suddenly asked, wanting to talk, rather than dwell on memories that could not help but make her sad.

Oh, how she missed her father.

"No eyes but my eyes have seen this pipe," Running Fox said solemnly, pausing from what he was doing. "Until you. And no one else will see it except for the one whom this is being made for."

Nancy's eyes widened. She was stunned by what he had just said.

"Who are you making it for?" she asked softly, wondering if she should even ask.

"Pipes are important in the transaction of important business," he said, not yet revealing a name to her. "Great labor and pride is taken in making and ornamenting pipes and pipe stems, especially those used on special occasions or presented to an important personage."

He paused and held the pipe out before him, the bowl resting in the palm of his right hand. "This pipe is made of red pipestone, and the stem, which is two feet long, was made of a young ash tree, the pith bored out with a wire," he said. He nodded toward the bowl. "As you see, the bowl of this pipe is not very large, but a single pipeful serves for ten or fifteen smokes, though in a company of men, especially old men, a pipe can be passed around at very short intervals."

"The feathers that hang from the stem are beautiful," Nancy murmured.

"I have only a few things more to do with the pipe and then it will be finished," Running Fox said, attaching more feathers at the base of the bowl. "I have worked on this special pipe where no one could see it, in my private lodge on Ghost Island. Soon the pipe will be used for the purpose it has been made for."

Nancy leaned forward, expecting him to tell her what fortunate person would be given such a special gift from someone as important as Running Fox, but instead, he set it aside, resting it on a thick pallet of buckskin.

He reached inside his parfleche bag, withdrew a much smaller pipe, and showed it to Nancy.

"Many Lakota maidens enjoy an occasional smoke," he said, causing Nancy to flinch. Was he going to ask her to smoke the pipe?

She watched breathlessly as he brought out a small pouch, then shook tobacco from it into the bowl.

After returning the pouch to his bag, he reached for a tiny piece of wood, held the tip in the flames of the fire until fire glowed on its end, then placed the pipe stem between his lips and lighted the tobacco.

He inhaled, then exhaled, sending a puff of smoke toward Nancy.

He stood and went around the fire and crouched beside her on his haunches. He held the pipe out for her until she, although hesitant, took it from him.

Her face grew hot with a blush as she gazed into his midnight-dark eyes. "What am I supposed to do with this?" she asked softly. "Surely you don't expect me—"

"It is something the Lakota women enjoy, as I believe you will," he said. He settled down beside her and crossed his legs in front of him.

He watched her still hesitating, then placed a

hand beneath her hand that held the pipe and lifted it up toward her mouth.

"Place the stem between your lips," he said encouragingly. "Inhale, but not too deeply, or the smoke from the pipe will be too warm for your lungs."

Feeling very awkward, even trapped, and having never seen any woman smoking a pipe before, Nancy cringed at knowing that she had no choice but to do as he asked, for she could tell that he was determined that she share smokes with him.

"What if I do inhale too deeply?" she blurted out, her pulse racing as she held the stem of the pipe closer to her lips.

But this was the first thing he had forced on her besides having made her leave the warmth of her bed.

He could have demanded many worse things of her, but he hadn't, and strangely enough she wanted to please him. She would take one puff on the pipe and hope that would be enough to satisfy him.

"Suck gently on the stem and that will be enough to bring smoke into your mouth," Running Fox said, watching her as she finally placed the stem between her lips. "We warriors inhale the smoke, drawing it into our lungs, then breathe it out through our nostrils. But you should just take it into your mouth and exhale again very quickly."

He watched as she took a whiff of the tobacco,

her eyes widening in wonder as it came into her mouth. Then, when she began coughing and gagging, he took the pipe from her and laid it aside.

Nancy fought to get air in her lungs, then forgot her discomfort when she felt his strong arms around her, holding her.

"Just relax," Running Fox said thickly, his heart pounding at the nearness of her.

He wanted her so badly, yet knew it was not the time to allow her to know his deep feelings for her.

The fact that she had trusted him enough to smoke the pipe told him more than mere words could say.

It was evident that she wanted to please him!

Nancy inhaled deeply, finally getting air into her lungs, then took this moment to revel in his nearness, his powerful arms so wonderful as he held her against him.

She so badly wished to twine her arms around his neck and tell him how she felt about him.

But she knew that she must not be so bold.

It would come naturally, if it was to come at all between them.

There would be no thought behind the kiss, the true embrace, the passion!

"I'm fine," she assured him, although she hated saying it because she knew that he would no longer · hold her. "Truly, I have finally gotten my breath again."

Reluctantly, he eased her from his arms, picked up the pipe, then sat down opposite from her again as he resumed working on the new pipe.

"I hope to meet with the Chippewa chief, Winter Moon, soon, to see if we can work together since young braves of our bands are involved in *min-newakan*, spirit water, problems," he explained. "The young braves are the princes of the wilderness. Their minds should not be clouded by spirit water. Thus far, the Chippewa chief, whose people have always been the *toka*—which in my language means 'enemy'—of the Lakota, hasn't agreed to such a meeting, and I wish that I didn't have to ask anything of the Chippewa. For so long they *have* been the Lakota's worst *toka*. But this is now. Things are different than in the past. Alliances are way more important than warring."

"Please tell me more about it," Nancy said, intrigued by what he had already told her. She had known that the Lakota and the Chippewa were ardent enemies—*toka*, as he had just taught her.

Yes, she had heard about the wars of long ago between the Lakota and the Chippewa, when each tried to annihilate the other. But she knew that there were now more important things for the two tribes to be concerned about. They had people like her stepfather, and the cavalry that was stationed in both Minnesota and Michigan, to be wary of.

"In the early 1840s, my Lakota people were

forced into a small corner of Minnesota land by the Chippewa," Running Fox said, laying his pipe aside.

He leaned forward and shoved another log into the flames of the fire, then settled back, his arms wrapped around his knees, as he looked over the fire at Nancy, glad that she did seem truly interested.

It was important that she know everything about his people, for he did hope that she would never leave and become a part of the white world again.

That world had treated her poorly.

He and his world had treated her with respect and caring.

"Under the leadership of my chieftain *ahte*, the Lakota word for 'father,' the Lakota signed a treaty in 1851 with whites, exchanging what was left of our Minnesota property for annuities, letting the Chippewa then have to deal with the whites, while we Lakota moved to another home along waters called Lake Michigan," he said. "Had I been chief I would not have given in to the Chippewa, or the whites. I would have fought for what was rightfully the Lakota's. But those who were in charge then, my father their leader, had not fought. The fight seemed gone from within them."

He paused, sighed, then said, "Now that my *ahte* is gone, as is my *ina*, mother, it is now my place to protect what my small band has left, and I will not sign any treaties which would take away from my people. But I also do not wish to make war with anyone to gain what I want."

Nancy listened as he continued talking. She was touched that he would share so much with her. To her, they grew closer as each moment passed.

"Now, I must place all old resentments toward the Chippewa aside in order to do what is best for both tribes' young braves, in order for the future of both tribes to be good, for the young braves are our peoples' future," he said. "I am proud to say that my people always have plenty of meat, as well as skins for the women to tan for moccasins and for repairing worn-out tepees, but we need much, much more than those things so that we can go to sleep every night at peace, and happy."

While Running Fox had been talking, he had taken the pipe up again and was decorating it with more feathers.

"This pipe will be a gift from myself to the Chippewa chief, Chief Winter Moon," Running Fox said.

Nancy now knew just how important the up-coming meeting was between these two powerful chiefs.

Chapter 10

It was another beautiful day, and Nancy marveled at how each day that passed drew her and Running Fox closer.

Today, he was showing her his horses. Nancy was struck by a well-muscled white steed whose eyes seemed to follow her.

"This one is so beautiful," she said, stroking the horse's withers.

"He is my favorite. His name is Ghost," Running Fox said. He smiled at Nancy when he heard a slight gasp. "You see the name as strange?"

"It's just that your island is called Ghost Island and now your horse is also called Ghost," Nancy said, pulling her hand away from the steed.

She gazed into Running Fox's eyes. "Why are there so many mysteries surrounding your people?" she asked guardedly. It might be taboo for him to discuss such things with her.

"Ghost Island is mysterious to those who do not understand its meaning," Running Fox said. He stepped away from Ghost and walked beside the corral.

"But we Lakota understand it," he said, turning toward her yet continuing to walk. "That is all that matters."

"The white people who know about your island are very, very afraid of it," Nancy said, walking beside him, her eyes also assessing the horses, finding them all muscled and lovely. Yet none compared with Ghost.

"And that is good," Running Fox said. He smiled at her. "We do not have to concern ourselves as much about white eyes coming to pry into our private business if they continue to be afraid."

He stopped, turned, and faced her. He gently placed his hands on her shoulders. "You are no longer afraid of the island *or* your reason for being here, are you?" he asked urgently, his eyes searching hers.

"No, and all because you and those who are on the island have given me no cause to be afraid," Nancy said, melting inside when she felt his hands on her shoulders. They were so tender, so natural, as though they belonged there.

Ghost suddenly whinnied and came up and

reached his nose out for Running Fox and nudged him in the side.

Running Fox turned to the horse and stroked his thick neck. "You want exercise, do you not, Ghost?" he asked. He glanced over at Nancy. "You said that you do not know how to ride. Would you want to learn today? Ghost is gentle."

"I don't know," Nancy said. She had always been afraid of horses after having seen her father thrown once from his steed, leaving him with a broken arm.

Even when his arm had healed, it had never been the same. It had always hung somewhat crooked.

The thought of her being injured in such a way, leaving her looking odd, made her shy away from wanting to ride today, if ever.

"The first time I saw that you had horses on the island I was puzzled," she said, sidestepping any more talk of her riding Ghost. "How did you get them to the island?"

"Each of them swam," Running Fox said, understanding that she was purposely avoiding any more mention of her riding today.

"Were you riding them as they swam?" Nancy asked incredulously. In her mind's eye she saw him looking proud and controlling as he led them through the water.

"*Ay-uh*, yes, I rode each of them, one by one,

until I had them in my corral," Running Fox said, walking toward the gate that led into the corral.

Nancy saw what he was up to—he was going to get Ghost.

She knew what to expect next.

He was truly not going to give up on her riding Ghost today.

Although she was still frightened, the thought of riding intrigued her. Surely with Running Fox there to control the horse, Ghost wouldn't throw her.

She again thought of her father. Even though he had been disfigured somewhat by his black steed, he had loved him no less afterward.

She would never forget watching him riding the horse, his long black hair flying in the wind behind him.

With his dark tan, and with that black hair and dark eyes, she had envisioned him to be a powerful Indian warrior—even then, she was intrigued by Indians. She and her father had found arrowheads in their garden, pointing to some tribe at some time in the past having lived where her family made their home.

She had always wondered which tribe it was, and whether a warrior's spirit had claimed her father on those days when he looked like one on the horse.

Surely it had been the Blackfoot, who even now made their homes in this same area.

She would never forget the look in her father's dark eyes when she had told him how she thought about him resembling a warrior. It was as though he had suddenly become that warrior, gazing intently at her.

And then he had thrown his head back in a loud laugh, swept her up into his arms, and carried her into their house for supper, teasing her all the while.

Then quickly the spell had been broken, and he had became her father again, tired from laboring all day in the fields and weary of any talk about anything.

"As other times, you are now so lost in thought," Running Fox said, drawing Nancy from her memories.

She smiled awkwardly at him. "I was thinking about my father . . . my *ahte*, and his love of horses," she replied.

"Your stepfather or your true father?" Running Fox asked guardedly, deeply touched that she had spoken a Lakota word instead of her own.

"My true *ahte*," Nancy said. "I miss him so much that sometimes my insides ache."

"As do I miss my *ahte* and *ina*," Running Fox said, placing reins on his horse. He glanced over at her. "Do you miss your *ina*, too? You never speak of her to me."

"My mother—my *ina*." Nancy sighed, as she

considered her torn feelings about her mother. She knew that her mother had disappointed her terribly by her marriage to Joseph Brock.

"Do you?" Running Fox asked, leading Ghost from the corral.

"Not as much as I miss my *ahte*," Nancy conceded. "And, anyway, *ina* is very much alive. *Ahte* is gone forever."

"You do not seem to truly miss her all that much," Running Fox said, while Ghost nibbled the fringe of his shirt.

"I do, but I can't allow myself to," Nancy said, then gulped hard when Running Fox slipped the reins into her hand.

She looked at the reins and then at him.

"It will be good for you to learn to ride," Running Fox said, his voice more serious than she had ever heard before.

Nancy wondered why he would feel this adamant about her riding, unless he saw it as a way to ensure her survival when she went back to live with her mother and stepfather.

If she could ride, she could decide to leave on her own.

But if Running Fox wanted her to learn for that reason, that meant that he truly was going to release her.

It meant that he did not want her to stay with him. But, Lord, that was what she wanted. She was finding such a beautiful peace inside her heart while with him.

"You do see my learning to ride as important, don't you?" Nancy asked, searching his eyes with hers. "Why?"

Sensing that she was trying to trap him into saying things that he was not ready to say, Running Fox said nothing more. Instead he placed his hands at her waist and quickly lifted her onto the horse, bareback.

Nancy's eyes widened as she gripped the reins. She was terrified at how unsteady she felt on Ghost. Without a saddle, she felt herself slipping sideways.

In a panic, she looked down at Running Fox. "I'm going to fall off," she cried.

"Use your knees to hold yourself steady," Running Fox said, placing a hand on her right knee, pressing it into Ghost's side. "See how doing so makes you feel more secure?"

Nancy pressed both of her knees into the horse's sides, smiling down at Running Fox when she finally felt steadied enough that she wouldn't slide off.

"Now nudge the horse with your knees instead of keeping them quiet," Running Fox said, nodding approvingly as Nancy did as he said, urging Ghost into a soft lope.

Running Fox ran alongside Ghost, his eyes not

leaving Nancy as she clung so tightly to the reins that her knuckles grew white.

"You are doing quite well," he encouraged. "Talk to Ghost. Make him your friend."

"What should I say?"

"Anything that comes to your mind."

Nancy gave Running Fox an awkward grin, then lowered her head and tried to think of something to say. "You are a pretty horse," she began, noticing how Ghost's ears pricked at her words. "You are also gentle. Can we be friends?"

She was stunned when he turned his head so that he could give her a quick glance with his huge and beautiful dark eyes. He nodded in a way that seemed to respond to her question!

"He understands what you said," Running Fox told her as Nancy glanced over at him. "He is your friend now, always and forever."

Nancy smiled bashfully. Then Running Fox grabbed the reins from her and stopped Ghost. "That is lesson enough for today," he said.

He helped her dismount, removed the reins from Ghost's back, then gently patted him on the rump, sending him off at a hard gallop.

Nancy watched the horse enjoying his freedom.

He would run, stop and whinny, glance at Running Fox and Nancy, then take off at a gallop again, his white mane flying in the wind.

"I have never seen such a beautiful sight,"

Nancy sighed, enchanted by the loveliness of Ghost as he romped, free and happy.

"And I truly enjoyed riding him," Nancy said, turning and smiling at Running Fox as he stood by her side.

"You shall ride again soon," Running Fox replied with a nod.

"Running Fox, I know that I should be wary of being your captive, but I'm not," Nancy told him. "I am anything but wary. I feel safe. I am happy for the first time since my father died."

She swallowed hard, then looked directly into his eyes. "In fact, you did me a favor by taking me from my life of tyranny," she said softly.

She sighed, lowered her eyes, then met Running Fox's gaze again. "And knowing my stepfather, he is probably glad that I'm gone. He still has my mother to do what I am no longer there to do. And he was getting fed up with my complaining. Mother never complains. So I am almost certain that my being gone works in his favor, not against it."

Running Fox's eyes widened. Had he not achieved anything at all by taking Nancy?

Perhaps what he had achieved was to have found a woman he loved!

But did she feel something special and intimate for him, too?

"Chief! Chief!"

A warrior broke the spell between Running Fox and Nancy.

Running Fox turned to see Gray Wolf, one of his warriors who had come from the main village, racing toward him.

Running Fox saw the concern—even panic—in Gray Wolf's eyes and knew that this warrior would not be there unless there was some sort of problem at the main village.

He broke into a run and met Gray Wolf halfway.

He placed a hand on his warrior's shoulder as Gray Wolf struggled to catch his breath. Nancy joined them.

"My chief, I have brought sad news to you about two of our young Lakota braves," Gray Wolf said as the women from the three tepees and their husbands came to see what the message was from the warrior. "Our braves met with some Chippewa braves. The Chippewa treated our Lakota braves to spirit water. Our Lakota youth arrived home at the main village, crazy and foolish."

Nancy felt guilt overwhelm her.

She hung her head, then felt a hand beneath her chin, tipping her head back. Her eyes met Running Fox's.

"You are not at fault here," Running Fox said slowly. "It is your stepfather who is at fault." He swallowed hard, his eyes taking on an angry gleam. "The young braves who participated in this, both Lakota and Chippewa, are also at fault. I must go to my main village to tend to the affair of our two braves. Then I will return to the island."

Nancy nodded and watched him walk away with Gray Wolf.

"*Hakamya-upo*, come with me," Soft Star murmured as she took Nancy by the hand. "You have admired my beadwork. Come to my lodge and I will teach you how it is done."

Nancy nodded, unable to speak. She was touched by the kindness of the woman who might have easily turned away from her.

She blinked back tears and followed Soft Star to her lodge.

"Choose which beads you like the most," Soft Star said as they both sat beside the fire.

Nancy tried to focus on learning, but she couldn't get her mind off Running Fox and what he might have to do to teach the two young braves just how bad it was to drink spirit water!

Chapter 11

At the main village, Running Fox stood in the council house with the two guilty braves.

The mothers of the two braves stood just outside the lodge, crying.

The fathers were inside the house with Running Fox, anger in their eyes and hearts.

"You have shamed your people today," Running Fox said as he looked from one drunk brave to the other. They were still so drunk, they couldn't stand steadily, and they giggled like two small girls caught doing something naughty.

Unable to stand the sight or the smell of the two braves, and realizing that his words were wasted on them while they were so drunk, Running Fox nodded at the fathers. "Each of you take your son and place him in a lodge by himself," he said tightly. "Tie them up until their evil spirits have gone away."

The young braves suddenly seemed to realize the anger of their chief, and they sobered up enough to beg for mercy.

This infuriated Running Fox. He pointed toward the entrance flap. "Go! Get out of my sight!" he shouted.

When he was alone in the council house, he sank down onto his haunches beside the fire, his eyes watching the flames lap away at the logs.

He was torn now as to what should be done about the Chippewa chief, for it was the Chippewa braves who had lured his Lakota braves into drinking spirit water when it had been denied them at their own homes.

He wasn't sure now if he should make overtures to Chief Winter Moon after all.

Would such an alliance work when that chief seemed to have no control whatsoever over his young braves?

Lately, there had been more than one incident involving Chippewa braves.

Remembering that an important ritual was to be held tomorrow, Running Fox made himself concentrate on that. There was to be a celebration of children, and several would get their ears pierced. It was not only an important ritual but quite an exciting day for their parents.

That was what this village needed now at a time when things had gone awry among its youth.

Ay-uh, yes—they needed tomorrow and all the fanfare that went with it.

By then, too, his young braves should have had plenty of time to think about the wrong they had done.

Their entire future was at stake, for if they continued to walk the wrong road of life, they would never be given the title of warrior!

Instead they would be banished from their homes forever.

Then his thoughts turned to Nancy.

He had a choice to make concerning her.

Should he request her presence at the ceremonies tomorrow, or leave her on the island?

While a part of him still warned him against getting involved with a white woman, that part of him that loved her made him decide to bring her to the ceremony.

She had opened up today and told him some things of her past, about a father she had loved with all of her heart. In return, he would share this important ritual, sacred to the Lakota, with her, the woman who had captured his heart.

Chapter 12

Nancy could hardly believe where she was. Early this morning Running Fox had asked her to accompany him to his main village for an ear-piercing ceremony of the children. He had not gone into why the ceremony was necessary; he just told her that it was.

Nor had he told her why he felt that it was necessary that she be there, but he had said enough that she knew she must be present.

She had reminded him that while she was there anyone could see her and know that he was responsible for her abduction.

He had responded that, in her new Indian attire, and with her hair no longer red, and worn in a long braid down her back, she would not be that noticeable should anyone come unexpectedly to his village.

Even her skin was tanned enough to fool anyone who would see her.

But then she had reminded him about her eyeglasses. With them on, she would definitely stand out from the others.

He had assured her that if his scouts came with news of anyone advancing on their village, she could remove the eyeglasses—or hide in a tepee.

Eager to join him, Nancy had done her best to put aside all doubts. She also tried to hide her excitement, for she still wasn't sure if it was wise to let him know just how happy she was to be with him.

This was a special day. Today she saw clearly the beauty of the Lakota's lodges and the lovely meadow near the lake. She recognized the sweet scent of burning cottonwood which filled the air.

She delighted in the sight of the grazing horses that dotted the green hillsides and admired the Indians, in their bright-colored clothes, who stood waiting for the ceremony to begin.

Later, the gathering in the council house was a true adventure for Nancy, as she observed the ear-piercing ceremony. She felt happy at the obvious pride of the parents whose children's ears were being pierced.

But she actually abhorred the practice. She had closed her eyes at the moment of each piercing, surprised that none of the girls cried out with pain as a tiny, sharp needle plunged through the tender flesh of their earlobes.

Afterward, when she opened her eyes again, she had noticed that the parents of the children whose ears were being pierced laid many beautiful pelts at the feet of the one who did the piercing.

When Running Fox saw her questioning look at the pelts being given so generously, he made his way to her side and explained that if those pelts were not given after the piercing, the child would not be considered as belonging to a family in good standing.

Nancy was glad when that part of the ceremony was over. Afterward those whose ears had been pierced proudly showed off the tiny bead earrings that had been placed in the holes in their ears.

Then there was much dancing, singing, and eating. Huge platters of food, bearing sliced venison roast, wild turnips, and berries, were passed around to those who wanted to eat.

Nancy let the platters go by, for she was absorbed in watching a cluster of children as they happily played various games.

Then her eyes widened when they all seemed to turn at the same time to stare at her.

As they began slowly advancing toward her, Nancy looked at Running Fox anxiously.

"I believe they are mystified by your eyeglasses," he said, just as the children stopped in front of them.

"My friends and I want to know what that strange contraption is on your nose," one of the girls blurted out. "When we look through the glass we see your eyes, yet when we look closely enough, we can see our reflection, like we see it when we look in the mirror of the lake."

"I was born to my parents with eyes that did not work as most people's work," Nancy tried to explain, feeling Running Fox's eyes on her. "So I have never been able to see as clearly as most people see. There are doctors who make eyeglasses, such as I am wearing today, that give one the ability to see again."

"How?" One of the children persisted.

Nancy swallowed hard, glanced over at Running Fox for support, then smiled at the children. "How? Like your shaman has the ability to make you well if you are ill or injured, the doctor who gave me the eyeglasses has the same sort of ability. He used the eyeglasses to doctor my eyes and I must wear them at all times if I am to see as well as you do without them."

One young brave stepped away from the others. "I would like to hold your eyeglasses," he said, reaching a hand out for them. "I would like to see if the same magic of your eyeglasses makes my eyes work better if I look through the glass as you do."

Nancy knew that if the child did look through her eyeglasses, he would not see better. In fact, everything would be a blur. She wasn't sure whether to allow him to find this out for himself or to try and talk him out of it.

"Should I?" she asked, turning quickly to Running Fox.

He smiled and nodded. "*Ay-uh,*" he said softly.

Nancy removed her eyeglasses and handed them to the child, holding her breath as he tried to put them on.

Another child took the eyeglasses from him, and then another, each peering through the glass and quickly handing the eyeglasses to the next child upon discovering that only a smeary blur was visible through them.

Running Fox's breath caught in his throat when he saw how carelessly the eyeglasses were being treated by one small girl. "Careful now, Tiny Doe," he said. "You are fumbling too much. You might drop the eyeglasses."

Nancy stiffened. "In which way is this child fumbling?" she asked guardedly, afraid her eyeglasses were going to be broken, yet unable to see for herself exactly what the problem was.

"Tiny Doe has always had trouble holding on to things," Running Fox said, glancing at Nancy. "She seems always to be more clumsy than the rest of the children."

Nancy's eyebrows forked. There was something very familiar about how Running Fox was describing this child. She recalled herself at a young age. She too was awkward and unable to do tasks that most children her age performed with ease.

No one knew why—until they discovered that she couldn't see as well as she should.

"This child," Nancy murmured. "How old is she?"

"Five winters of age," Running Fox said.

"Running Fox, will you do something for me?" Nancy inquired.

"What would you ask of me?" Running Fox asked, distracted by watching Tiny Doe, who still fumbled awkwardly with the eyeglasses yet did not seem all eager to give them to the next child.

"Put the eyeglasses on that child," Nancy softly suggested.

Running Fox glanced questioningly at Nancy, then seeing nothing so wrong in what she requested, he gently placed the eyeglasses on Tiny Doe's nose.

Nancy heard how the little girl suddenly gasped and hoped that the gasp was for the right reason.

"I can see things!" Tiny Doe cried. "I can finally see more than light and shadow!"

Tears came to Nancy's eyes, for she knew that

this young girl was seeing clearly for the first time in her life.

It touched Nancy's heart to know that she might be able to help someone the same way she had been helped so long ago by the doctor who had discovered her problem.

She started to tell Running Fox, but stopped when another voice, the voice of a jealous child, spoke up.

"Let me see them," said Blue Wing, a child of Tiny Doe's age, as he yanked the eyeglasses from her.

And just as Blue Wing took them, he dropped them.

The eyeglasses hit a large rock and the glass lenses shattered.

Gasps rippled from child to child, and then there was an awkward silence.

Running Fox knew that Nancy wasn't aware yet of what had happened.

"What is it?" Nancy asked, feeling around her. "What happened?"

"Your eyeglasses are broken," Running Fox said, knowing that the news couldn't be worse for Nancy, for without her eyeglasses, she didn't really have eyes with which to see.

Nancy's heart plummeted.

She was too stunned to say anything.

"Nancy, how can I help?" Running Fox asked softly. He placed a gentle hand on her cheek. He was amazed that she hadn't gotten angry and scolded the one who broke her eyeglasses.

Blue Wing stepped up to Nancy. His eyes were focused on the ground. "I am sorry," he said, his voice breaking. "I did not mean to break them."

"I know," Nancy said softly. She reached her arms out and hugged the child. "It's okay. I know it was an accident. If you will, though, please pick up the remains of my eyeglasses and bring them to me. But be careful. Don't cut your fingers with the glass."

Anxious to help, Blue Wing fell on his knees, swept up what remained of her eyeglasses, and took it all back to her.

"*Hiye-pila-maya*, thank you," Nancy said in the Indian language she knew would be best used now, at such an awkward time. She had always been a quick learner, and she was glad that worked in her favor now.

Blue Wing placed the frames and larger bits of glass into her outstretched palm.

Nancy sighed. "Running Fox, there is one man who can help. Doc Harris. He is the one who supplies me with my eyeglasses. He always keeps a spare pair on hand should I break the ones I have. Will you please take me to him? Doc Harris won't tell my stepfather I have been there. He sympathizes with me and hates the kind of life my stepfather forced on me."

Running Fox studied her face, hoping that she wasn't trying a tactic that would, in the end, bring harm to his people because of his decision to abduct her.

"Running Fox, all I want is to be able to see again," Nancy said in a rush when she realized that he was hesitating. "Honestly, Running Fox, I won't cause you any problems by going to Doc Harris's, nor will he, if I explain how things are. He is a dear man who will only want what is best for me."

"And he will see you being with a man with red skin is best?" Running Fox said as everyone stood by, listening and watching.

"At this moment in time, yes," Nancy said clearly. She reached out until she found his hand, then held it. "You have to know that I could never do anything to bring harm to you or your people. You do, don't you?"

"I took you from your bed and made you my captive," Running Fox said hesitantly.

"I know, but I hardly feel like a captive. You surely know that, Running Fox. Surely you know that."

Running Fox gazed into her eyes, realizing how little she could see without the aid of her eyeglasses and knowing that he would risk anything now to make her whole again.

"I will take you," Running Fox said gravely. "I

will send a scout to arrange a meeting between you and Doc Harris."

"Do you know him?" Nancy asked in surprise.

"All know of his kindness, even we Lakota," Running Fox said. He nodded at one of his scouts. "Go. Do as I have promised."

The scout nodded, then ran to his horse, mounted it, and rode away.

"*Hakamya-upo*, come with me," Running Fox said, taking her gently by an arm. "I will take you to my lodge."

Nancy held on to his hand and went with him to his tepee while the merriment resumed behind them.

After getting settled inside Running Fox's tepee, Nancy could only see the color of the fire in the firepit, but could not make out any shapes.

She hated not being able to see Running Fox, but she felt him all around her—his manly smell, his presence that she had begun to revel in.

Running Fox sat beside her, in his mind recalling the moment Nancy had realized that her eyeglasses had been broken.

He was still amazed that she hadn't gotten angry and scolded the one who broke them. Instead she had hugged the child. Running Fox had felt her kindness in his own heart.

He was in love with her, ah, so deeply in love with her!

"Doc Harris can be trusted," Nancy assured him. "He will want what is best for me, and once he sees that you haven't harmed me, he will know that I'm all right. He knows how much I loathed being under my stepfather's thumb."

When he didn't respond, Nancy wondered if she had reminded him that abducting her had not gained him anything, since her stepfather did not care one iota that she was gone.

Chapter 13

Doc Harris stood beneath an oak tree. He was tall and lanky, with a head of thick gray hair, his eyes squinting through his dark-rimmed eyeglasses as he fitted Nancy with her new pair.

When she could see her old friend, the doctor, standing there, watching her, she flung herself into his arms. "Thank you," she cried. "Oh, thank you so much for coming with my spare eyeglasses."

He returned her hug as he peered over her shoulder at Running Fox.

Running Fox stiffened, for he could see things in this doctor's eyes that made him uncomfortable. Although Nancy had promised that the man could be trusted, Running Fox had some lingering doubts.

But he had had no choice but to take a chance, for he knew the importance of Nancy's having eyeglasses. When he gazed at her, he did not want her just to see movement and shadows. He wanted her to see him, so that she would know, without a doubt, that he truly cared for her as a woman, a woman whom he no longer saw as his captive.

He had finally let down his guard and allowed himself to feel what he had fought against for so long.

He was in love with this woman, heart and soul.

And by the way she turned now and gazed into his eyes, he knew that they had long ago gone beyond captor and captive.

"I can see," she exclaimed, stepping away from Doc Harris.

She sighed and clasped her hands as she turned and smiled at the doctor.

"I truly appreciate what you have done for me today."

"How could I not?" Doc Harris said, taking her hands in his. "You're my little Nancy."

Nancy blushed and lowered her eyes, then smiled at Doc Harris again.

Her smile faded as she searched his eyes with hers. "Please don't tell my stepfather," she said, her voice breaking.

"I told you that I wouldn't," Doc Harris said. "I understand why you want to be away from your stepfather." He shifted his gaze to Running Fox, held it steady there for a moment, then looked into

Nancy's eyes once again. "I just can't understand why you feel comfortable about having actually been abducted from your bed."

"Yes, in most cases a woman would be uncomfortable about that," she conceded. She smiled at Running Fox, then looked again at Doc Harris. "But this man, this Lakota chief, actually did me a favor by taking me not only from my bed, but also from a life of tyranny forced upon me by my stepfather. I am finally free."

She stepped away from Doc Harris and stood beside Running Fox. "Running Fox abducted me, but he never meant to harm me," she said softly. "He did it to get back at Joe for not heeding his warnings about selling whiskey to the young Lakota and Chippewa braves. Words had not worked. He had hoped that action would."

"But you are being used as a pawn," Doc Harris said, looking from Nancy to Running Fox. "No matter how you look at it, that should not have happened."

"Perhaps not. But as you see, I am safe and happy. And all because of Running Fox."

Doc Harris squinted through his own eyeglasses again as he searched Running Fox's eyes. "Son, I trust that you will continue to treat my little Nancy with kindness," he said cautiously. "And when she is ready to leave, I would hope that you would allow it. You've made your point with the whiskey peddler. I'm certain he has learned from it."

"Not entirely," Running Fox said heavily. "He still makes his whiskey runs, but he is more careful now where he goes and with whom he tries to make trade."

"Then what will your next move be if abducting an innocent woman is not enough to convince him that you mean business?" Doc Harris asked, sliding his hands into the front breeches pockets of his dark suit.

"That will be discussed in council between me and my warriors," Running Fox answered. "In time, the whiskey peddler will be stopped."

"And you say Running Fox has been treating you with kindness?" Doc Harris asked, shifting his focus to Nancy.

"Much," Nancy replied, glancing at Running Fox.

"Then God be with you both," Doc Harris said, nodding. "I am not a man of prejudice, so I do wish you well, Running Fox."

Running Fox stepped away from Nancy and her eyes widened when he embraced Doc Harris.

"Thank you for helping Nancy, and for your trust in me," Running Fox said. Then he stepped away from the doctor and grasped his horse's reins. His white steed stood next to the horse Nancy would ride back to the village. She had ridden with Running Fox to meet Doc Harris, with plans to ride the other steed back to the village after she had gotten her eyeglasses.

Running Fox untied Ghost's reins and handed them to Nancy.

"Do you think I have learned enough about riding to make it all the way back to the village?" Nancy asked, her pulse racing at the thought of actually being on the horse alone for that distance.

"You are an excellent enough rider to go far on the steed," Running Fox said, smiling at Nancy as she took the reins. "You have proven to me that you were born to be on a horse."

The spell that had just begun to weave itself between her and Running Fox almost made them forget they had an audience until Doc Harris cleared his throat.

"Nancy, I've brought an extra pair of eyeglasses for you," he said, holding out a leather case to her.

"Why?" Nancy asked, taking them. "Why are you giving me two pairs today instead of one?"

"To keep you from putting yourself in danger a second time by venturing this close to Dry Gulch should you break your newest pair," he said, gently patting Nancy on the arm.

"I will place the second pair in my parfleche bag," Running Fox said as Nancy handed them to him.

Nancy turned to Doc Harris and gave him another hug.

"Again, thank you for what you have done

today," she murmured. "Thank you for being so thoughtful."

"Anytime you need me for anything, Nancy, I will help you," Doc Harris said, easing himself from her arms. He gently framed her face between his wrinkled old hands and smiled into her violet eyes. "My sweet little Nancy."

She blushed, smiled, then watched him mount his steed and waved at him as he rode away.

Once he was out of sight, Nancy turned to Running Fox. "I can see you again."

He smiled, then took her hand as they walked towards her horse.

After helping her into the saddle, he stood there for a moment longer, gazing into her violet eyes as she looked back at him. Then he mounted Ghost.

"We had best head back home," he said seriously. "It is not good for you to be gone for this length of time this far from my people. Your stepfather could be on a whiskey run, which would take him across our path. It is best for him that that does not happen."

Nancy's brow clouded, for she would have thought that Running Fox's main concern would be her stepfather spotting her with the young chief.

Then what he surely meant sank in. If her stepfather saw her with Running Fox, Running Fox would have no choice but to silence him—or take him captive.

She didn't want to think that Running Fox would be capable of murdering her stepfather. If he was, surely he would have already done it.

They headed out in the direction of the village.

Nancy was so proud that she had been able to learn how to ride a horse so quickly.

Beneath the warmth of the sun, with the wind soft and smooth against her face, she felt her spirits soar.

A general sense of well-being and happiness swam through her, something that she had not felt for a long time, since her father had died and her family had been torn apart by his death.

But today, everywhere she looked she saw all sorts of wildflowers, a feast for the senses, a sweet and intoxicating fragrance of nature's perfume. Everything about today would be savored and remembered. Nancy was delighted when they entered a great field of golden sunflowers. Beneath the brilliant rays of the sun, the leaves shone bright and green, and the yellow petals were more lovely and delicate than gold—a true sea of color.

Many little birds hovered over the sunflowers, picking at the seeds, their feathers almost as yellow as the flowers' petals neatly arranged around the centers of brown.

"I have never seen anything quite as beautiful as that," Nancy said, looking at Running Fox, whose own eyes were on the flowers and the hovering birds.

"There was a time when buffalo roamed freely on the land and could be seen among the sunflowers," Running Fox said. "They liked to wallow their big heads in the flowers, and some would have long stems wound about their horns as though they were meant to be there."

"That would be wonderful to see," Nancy said, trying to envision buffalo there.

"The buffalo are few now, and no longer a staple food for my people," Running Fox said gravely. "Like so many other parts of Lakota life long ago, the buffalo were taken by whites. All red men had to find other means of food, lodge coverings, and other things the buffalo lent to the lives of the Indian."

After one more look at the sunflowers, Nancy rode on with Running Fox.

She peeked at her companion, expecting to see bitterness in his eyes after being reminded of what the white man had taken from him and his people.

Instead she saw a gentle peace on his face and in his eyes as he turned to her and smiled.

He held nothing against her because of what others were capable of doing against him and his people.

"You are more beautiful than any flower that grows beneath the sun," Running Fox said, as a strange sort of warm, sensual feeling spread through Nancy.

She wasn't sure how to reply, for he had more or less told her that he loved her!

She was glad when the village came into view. She did not want to say anything yet. She wanted the words to be just right when she confessed her feelings to him.

Running Fox dismounted, then took her horse's reins.

"Come with me inside my lodge," he said, their eyes locking.

She dismounted and watched as a young brave came and took both horses away to Running Fox's corral.

"Shouldn't we get back to the island?" she asked.

"You are now a part of my main lodge, not my secondary one," Running Fox said. He stood there, his eyes on her. "I can tell this is where you would wish to be. It was in your eyes as soon as the eyeglasses were placed on your nose and you gazed at me in such a wondering and loving way. You wished to be with me. It was then that I knew that our hearts are now as one."

Chapter 14

Afraid that the people of the village might notice her hesitating to enter Running Fox's lodge, Nancy hurried past him, then watched him lower the flap and turn to her.

"You said that you knew that our hearts are now as one," she said, trying not to show how her heart was throbbing inside her chest.

"*Ay-uh*, yes. Like I said, it became known to me when your eyeglasses were placed on your nose and our eyes met and held," Running Fox said.

He stepped up in front of her.

He placed his hands on her cheeks and gazed more intently into her violet eyes.

"You looked at me in such a wondering, loving way," he said. "It was apparent that you had missed seeing me while you had no eyeglasses to see through. When you could see, I saw everything in your eyes that spoke of your feelings toward me. You had missed me, as I had missed knowing that you could see how I felt about you."

"I do feel so much for you," Nancy said shyly. "At first I was afraid to, but now—"

"But now?" he said, interrupting her when he saw how hard it was for her to say her true feelings. "You do love me. You want me as I want you."

He placed a hand beneath her chin. "Say it," he said huskily. "*Mitawin*, my woman, tell me that you love me—that you want me."

Nancy felt a rush of warmth sweep through her.

She knew this was caused by needs never felt by her before.

She *did* want him.

And, no, she had never wanted a man before, especially not like this.

But how could she tell him?

The words were difficult to say, for wouldn't they reveal to him that she wanted to make love?

"I do love you," she said, feeling heat rush to her cheeks.

She had just admitted to him that she loved him!

"Do you need me?" Running Fox asked, leaning his face closer to hers. "Say it if you feel it. Do you need me?"

Nancy swallowed hard, for once she said it she could not take the words back.

"I am so grateful to you for having taken me from a life that I feel would have had a terrible ending. Sooner or later one of those drunken men at the Crystal Palace would have . . ."

She drew a shaky breath. "One of them could have accosted me," she finished. "I would not have been able to live with myself had that happened. I would have probably even taken my own life."

"Do not say such a thing, or ever think it again," Running Fox said. He wrapped his arms around her and drew her close.

Then another thought came to him.

He gently placed his hands on her shoulders and eased her away from him so that they could look into each other's eyes. "Are you saying things that you feel about me because you feel grateful to me?" he asked, searching her eyes. "You love me for me, do you not? Not for what I have done for you?"

She reached up to touch his cheek.

"No," she said, smiling. "I am not saying that I love you and want you because I feel grateful. I love you, not for what you did, but for who you are. I have never loved before. I have never wanted a man before. But now I do! I want you with every beat of my heart."

Gently Running Fox took her eyeglasses from her nose and laid them aside. He was aflame with spiraling needs when he lifted her into his arms and carried her back to his bed of blankets and pelts.

He kissed her, his mouth urgent and eager.

Overwhelmed with sweet longings so new to her, Nancy twined her arms around Running Fox's neck.

Her lips quivered as his kiss deepened, his hands between them now, caressing her breasts through the soft doeskin dress.

A surge of ecstasy raged through Nancy, stunning her at the wonders of his kiss and caresses.

She sucked in a wild breath of pleasure when Running Fox placed a knee between her legs and pressed gently upward against her private place, where strange stirrings were being awakened.

Realizing that she was experiencing sensations completely new to her, Running Fox gazed into her face.

"You have never made love before?" he asked huskily.

"No," Nancy said shyly, hating that she couldn't see him clearly.

But his hands were there, and so were his lips and his voice.

They were all that she needed.

"Are you ready to make love, or would you rather wait?" Running Fox asked, although he was on fire with need of her.

"I don't think I could bear waiting," Nancy said,

swallowing hard. "The way you touch me . . . the way you kiss me . . ."

"The way I love you?" Running Fox said, again pressing gently between her thighs, where he knew her desires were truly centered.

He heard her quick intake of breath.

"Yes, the way you love me," Nancy said. He knelt beside her and slowly drew her dress over her head, then removed her moccasins.

"Oh, I do wish that I could see you," she murmured when she heard the rustle of clothes and knew that he was undressing himself.

He could tell that she was trying to see him more clearly through the blur of her eyes.

Totally nude, he reached a hand out and took one of Nancy's. "Touch me, feel me," he said, placing her hand on his chest. "As you explore my body with your hands, just know that it is yours, only yours, forever."

Her pulse raced as she slowly ran her hands over his chest, which was bare of hair, and then over the corded muscles of his shoulders. Gently, she stroked one of his arms, and then moved it to his flat belly.

She heard his quick intake of breath, and she felt his belly quiver at her touch. He took one of her hands and lowered it on him until she felt . . .

His manhood.

It was large and tight to the touch, and when he

urged her to move her hand on him, she could feel the heat growing inside him and could even feel a pulse beat, like his heart might be centered there.

Feelings overwhelmed her as she continued to explore his body, especially when she heard him breathing harder, as though he was taking much pleasure from what she was doing.

Then suddenly he took her hand away and placed it on herself, between her thighs, where thick tendrils of dark curls covered that most private part of her body.

She could feel the blush rush to her cheeks when he urged her to move her hand on herself.

Then her breath quickened, and Running Fox quickly replaced her hand with his own.

As he caressed her with his warm fingertips, she felt the heat rising within her, as though someone had set a candle close by and was moving its warmth closer to her body.

She closed her eyes and tossed her head back and forth as the pleasure built within her. Then she was aware of something else being where his hand had just been.

She felt his manhood there, gently probing where no man had ever been before.

Her breath caught as he pushed himself slowly inside her. Then she gasped with pain when he went farther and seemed to have torn away some flesh within her.

She opened her eyes, cursing silently to herself while wanting so badly to look into his eyes, to question him with her own.

But his lips kissed her passionately as he pressed endlessly deeper inside her, then withdrew and entered again, this time with no pain accompanying it. Instead, pure ecstasy flooded Nancy, and she closed her eyes and felt herself engulfed in euphoria as a surge of tingling heat coursed through her body.

"You are feeling so much that is new to you," Running Fox whispered against her lips. "Is it all good?"

"It is very, very good," Nancy whispered back, the spinning sensations within her rising up and flooding her whole body, pushing at the very boundaries of who she was.

Again he kissed her, as each of his thrusts inside her sent messages to her heart that she would remember forever.

She clung to him.

She twined her legs around his waist, as though practiced in loving him back in such a way.

It was such a splendid joy that she was experiencing, an awakening that she had never known existed between men and women.

When he reached between their bodies and molded one of her breasts with his hand, she gasped with the pleasure that he caused.

Her hand swept down his spine in a soft caress.

He held her tightly as their bodies strained together hungrily.

A cry of sweet agony escaped Nancy's lips as bliss overcame her, their bodies jolting and quivering as each found ultimate pleasure.

Then Running Fox rolled away from Nancy and closed his eyes, his pulse racing, his body still quivering with the pleasure that he had just found with the woman he would love forever.

Nancy was amazed at what she had just experienced. She had always heard that making love was something one could not describe, that one had to do it to understand its full glory.

She now knew!

She stared in wonder at Running Fox. She caressed his cheek. "I love you," she murmured.

He reached for her hand and kissed its palm. "I shall never love anyone but you," he said, then drew her against him and held her endearingly close. "My *mitawin*, my Nancy, I will always protect you. Always."

She inscribed those words on her heart, knowing that he meant them.

He had not only given her back her life, but he had also given her his love!

The sound of approaching footsteps interrupted her thoughts. "I have brought food," Soft Star said, speaking through the closed entrance flap.

Nancy sat up abruptly, embarrassed that she had nothing on.

She had also just made love.

Could one tell it by looking?

If Soft Star saw her now, would she know?

She was surprised to hear Soft Star's voice, since she had thought that Soft Star would still be on the island during her husband's time of standing guard there.

She grabbed her dress and hurried into it as Running Fox pulled on his own clothes.

"Leave the food outside, beside the entrance," Running Fox said, knowing that Nancy would be more comfortable if she didn't have to come face-to-face with another woman after making love.

"It is something I made special for you after seeing that you are back home," Soft Star said. "And it is good to be back in my main lodge, Chief Running Fox."

Then Nancy heard soft footsteps walking away.

She sat beside the fire as Running Fox retrieved the pot of food, brought it inside the lodge, and hung it on the spit over the fire.

"Soft Star and her husband are no longer on the island?" she asked, her mouth watering at the tantalizing aroma of the venison stew.

"He will remain at the main village until a full moon comes again, and then he and Soft Star will return to the island," Running Fox said as he got two wooden bowls and spoons, then came and sat beside Nancy again.

He smiled as he picked up her eyeglasses and placed them on her nose. "Now you can see again," he said, leaning close to kiss her.

"I do not need eyes to see when I can feel so much," Nancy sighed, nodding a thank-you to him as he gave her a bowl of steaming stew.

Running Fox sat beside her with his own bowl of stew. "I feel many things tonight," he said, glancing through the smoke hole overhead, where the moon had replaced the sun in the sky.

"As do I," Nancy said, blushing. She gazed up at the dark heavens as well, then smiled over at Running Fox. "The night is new."

"And long," he said, chuckling.

"That is good," Nancy said, peering over the spoon at Running Fox as she sucked a piece of onion between her lips. Their eyes met knowingly.

He laughed huskily.

Chapter 15

Nancy smiled into the flames of the fire. Had anyone told her that her life would ever be changed this much, even a few months ago, she would have scoffed.

Her smile faded as she remembered the horrors of her old life.

Her life since the death of her father had been something akin to living in the pits of hell.

"I have been watching your eyes as you are in such deep thought," Running Fox said, trying to draw her attention away from her unpleasant memories.

She looked quickly over at him and saw deep concern in his midnight-dark eyes. "I was thinking about how my life was before you came in the dark of the night and swept me away from it," she blurted out.

She wiped a tear from the corner of an eye.
"Running Fox, because of you it has all changed,"
she murmured. "It's like . . . like I have been reborn."

Running Fox's eyes widened in wonder.

He lifted her onto his lap, facing him. "As have
I," he said huskily. He brushed soft kisses across
her lips. "Because of you I am now a fulfilled man.
Until you, my *mitawin*, I was only partially alive.
Now I too feel, as you say, reborn. You have
brought to me something rare between two people—a love so pure and true that everything within
me feels at peace. You complete me, Nancy. My
sweet and beautiful Nancy."

Nancy reached her hands to his face and framed
it between them. "As do you, my Running Fox,"
she whispered. "Even when I could not see you in
the dark, I knew it was you and was glad. I never
feared what you asked of me. I knew that you were
there to change my life, and I knew it would be for
the better. I was so glad to leave that place."

"How could you know that I would not harm
you, that you could trust me so completely?" Running Fox asked, searching her eyes.

"Although I could never see you while I was
with my stepfather on the whiskey runs, your voice
told me what sort of person you were," Nancy explained. "Although you had every reason to hate
my stepfather, even to kill him, you spoke in gentle

tones to him and allowed him his freedom when you could have forced him into captivity. I admired you from that first moment I heard your kind and gentle voice. I wished then that I could see you. I wanted to see the face that matched that voice and gentle heart."

"And now you have," Running Fox said as Nancy gently ran her fingers over his face, as though touching it for the first time.

"Yes, and now I have. Running Fox, I want to be with you always. I feel something within me that I haven't felt since my father's death. I feel protected, loved, and at peace with myself. Thank you, my love. Thank you."

Gently, meditatively, he removed her eyeglasses and laid them aside, then lifted her into his arms and carried her back to their bed of blankets and pelts.

Soon they were making love again.

When he sank his manhood into her, she heard his thick, husky groan as she let out a soft cry of passion.

He gave her a meltingly hot kiss, causing the pleasure to spread through her body in searing splashes.

She twined her arms around his neck and clung to him and gave herself up to the rapture.

Waves of liquid heat pulsed through Running

Fox's body as he reached between them and slid a hand around one of her breasts, cupping it.

Then he leaned down and showered heated kisses over her taut-tipped breasts.

His hot breath tickled her breasts, and his tongue was wet and warm against the nipples as he licked one and then the other.

His hands took in the roundness, and his tongue brushed the nipples ever so lightly.

Again he kissed her.

Nancy could feel the hunger in the hard, seeking pressure of his lips against her own.

She ran her hand down his muscled back and then clung tightly to him when she felt the pleasure rising up within her, spreading and swelling until it blotted out all other sensations.

Overcome with his own feverish heat, his steel arms enfolding her, Running Fox made one last plunge inside her and then held her tightly against him as they both reached that place of euphoria where ecstatic waves of sheer bliss carried them away.

Running Fox closed his eyes, then opened them again when Nancy brushed soft kisses across his brow, and then his lips.

"My love," she whispered, thrilling through and through when he reached between her thighs and gently caressed her where she was still tender from lovemaking.

But the tenderness seemed to enhance the pleasure that he was once again arousing within her.

She closed her eyes and allowed it to happen again, then sucked in a wild breath of ecstasy when she felt something wet where his fingers had just been and knew that she was experiencing yet another new sensation tonight, a different way for him to give her pleasure. He was making love to her with his mouth, tongue, and lips, where she would have thought no man should go.

Her womanhood pulsed heatedly beneath his caresses, so much so that she could not openly question what he was doing. She could only enjoy the wonders of it.

She gasped and tossed her head back and forth as the pleasure mounted and then exploded within her and spread like wildfire throughout her, as once again tonight she was taken to paradise and back.

Enjoying having given her pleasure again, Running Fox lay beside her, his hands running through her hair, his eyes taking in the loveliness of her tiny body.

"What you just did . . . ," Nancy said, opening her eyes, blushing.

"There are many ways to receive and give pleasure when two people are in love," Running Fox said, again placing his hand where he had just made love to her. He stroked gently, causing her breath to catch.

"But what you just did . . . ," Nancy said again, wishing she could see more than shadow and movement as he sat up beside her, reached for a blanket, and wrapped it around her as she sat up.

"What I just did was love you," he said simply.

He lifted her into his arms and carried her over to the warmth of the fire.

"I need my eyeglasses," she said. "I want to see you. I want to feast my eyes upon you."

He found them and placed them on her nose.

Nancy smiled as she reached out and touched his cheek gently. "If only I could see all of the time," she mused. "I would love seeing you during love-making, how your expressions change. It would be wonderful to see you at the moment of total bliss, how your eyes would surely darken with plea-sure."

"You have a vivid imagination," Running Fox said, chuckling.

"I have needed to because I have not always had my eyes to depend on," Nancy said, laughing softly. "I wish that no one had to have the same af-fliction as I. Sometimes I feel less than whole be-cause of my poor eyesight."

Then she moved into his arms. "Until you, that is," she said softly. "While I am with you, with or without my eyeglasses, I feel so whole, so complete."

Then she sat back, her eyes wide, a sudden excitement in her heart. "Running Fox, there is someone in your village who has the same empty feelings that I have always had when I have not had my eyeglasses on. The little girl, Tiny Doe—the one who could see so much better after she tried my eyeglasses. Running Fox, Doc Harris gave me two pairs of eyeglasses. I need only one, and should that pair break, he has another ready for me."

"What are you saying?" Running Fox asked.

"I want to give my spare eyeglasses to Tiny Doe," Nancy explained. "Although they more than likely won't be the exact prescription, it was obvious when she put them on that they helped her. They helped her see better immediately."

"Prescription?" Running Fox asked, perplexed. "I am unfamiliar with that word."

Nancy explained what it meant, then looked anxiously into his eyes. "What do you think? Do you think the child's mother would allow her to wear my eyeglasses? When your people first saw them they called them a contraption. But when they saw how they helped Tiny Doe see, they were in awe. Surely she would be allowed to wear them."

Running Fox drew Nancy into his arms. Their eyes met. "My *mitawin*, more and more I see you as a woman of heart," he said joyously. "I want all of my people to see it in you. Tomorrow I will call a special council for everyone to witness you giving the eyeglasses to the child."

Nancy's eyes wavered. "I'm not the sort of person who craves to be the center of attention," she said, swallowing hard. "I hated those moments on-stage when all eyes were on me. Wouldn't this be almost the same?"

But even as she asked him that question, she knew that this was the perfect time for her to get past the awkward shyness that had plagued her all of her life.

"Yes, I'll do it," she said softly.

"*Hakamya-upo*, come here," Running Fox said, reaching out for her.

She went to him and reveled in his touch as he hugged her close to him.

"You will make Tiny Doe very happy tomorrow," he said, then brushed kisses across her lips. "As you make me happy now."

Chapter 16

Nancy stood at the back of the council house.

She understood why Running Fox was making a big issue out of this, needing everyone present—it was because no one of his band had ever worn eyeglasses. They were something worn by white people, not Indians.

Nancy glanced at Tiny Doe as she sat with her mother, who already knew the purpose of this council. Running Fox had told Nancy that Tiny Doe's mother was uneasy about what would be offered to her daughter today, yet she did remember seeing how the eyeglasses had helped Tiny Doe when the little girl had briefly worn Nancy's. She was trying to adjust to the idea that her daughter would from now on look different from the other children.

But Tiny Doe would also be able to play and enjoy games that she only half enjoyed now since she could never truly participate. She had always been clumsy, and she usually dropped out of the games and stood back, alone, trying to see what was happening.

Nancy gazed over at Running Fox, who was standing beside her. She could see some tightness in his jaw as he watched his people coming in. She knew that he was somewhat uneasy about what was about to happen.

"Some of my people are skeptical about what we have planned, but more are understanding and want what is best for Tiny Doe," he said. "They have all seen her struggling because of her poor eyesight. She told me a moment ago that she is very excited about being able to learn beading from her mother once she can see, even more than about playing games with friends. She has only been able to feel the beads, not see them. She will be in wonder of the bright colors at last."

"I'm so glad things seem to be working out for her," Nancy cried. "I had been so afraid that more people would be against her receiving the eyeglasses than would support her, for I know resentment toward the habits of whites runs strong among all Indian tribes. I have seen resentment in the eyes of some of your people when they see me, especially when I am with you. Will that ever change?"

"In time," Running Fox said. "They have experienced so much that was bad from the white community, it is hard for them to trust any white people. But they trust their chief, and in time all will see you as one of them, because you will be their chief's wife."

Nancy's eyes widened.

Her heart soared. Had she truly heard him say that she would be his wife?

"*Ay-uh*, my wife," he said, as though he had read her thoughts. "Soon, my *mitawin*. Soon."

"Nothing would make me happier," Nancy murmured, then turned from him as Tiny Doe and her mother came to stand before them.

Suddenly Tiny Doe stepped behind her mother, causing Nancy's breath to catch in her throat. Had the child changed her mind?

"Tiny Doe?"

Running Fox's gentle voice reached Tiny Doe, causing her to move slowly back to her mother's side.

"It is time, Tiny Doe, to accept the gift of the eyeglasses from Nancy," Running Fox said.

Nancy stepped forward. She took the eyeglasses from the case. "The case is also yours," she explained as she held it out to Tiny Doe.

Her mother, instead, took it, for it was obvious

that Tiny Doe couldn't see the case well enough to take it.

Nancy turned to the woman. "When she is not wearing the eyeglasses they can be kept safely within the case."

Tiny Doe's mother nodded, then knelt down beside Tiny Doe and placed a gentle hand on her child's cheek. "It is time now, Daughter, to allow the white woman to place the eyeglasses on your nose," she said softly. "Remember that it is being done so that you can see as well as all of your friends."

Tiny Doe nodded. "I would like to wear the eyeglasses," she said shyly. "I enjoyed seeing your face, Mother, and faces of my friends, when I wore them before. I will also enjoy seeing butterflies, the sky, and tiny animals that I have not been able to see."

She smiled as Nancy knelt down before her and slowly placed the eyeglasses on her nose.

She soon discovered they were somewhat too large.

But Nancy knew how to fix that.

"They are too large for you, so I must make an adjustment," she said as she took the eyeglasses from Tiny Doe's nose. "I shall bend the wire just a little bit and then the eyeglasses should fit snugly enough on you so that they won't fall off when you play games with your friends."

After bending the frames so that they fit Tiny Doe's smaller face, Nancy once again placed them on the child.

She held her breath, for Tiny Doe had yet to say anything. The child gazed intently through the lenses, reaching up and touching the glass wonderingly.

"Daughter, can you see better?" her mother asked as she knelt down beside Nancy, who was still waiting for Tiny Doe's reaction.

Suddenly Tiny Doe laughed in merriment. She reached out and ran her fingers over her mother's face, and then over Nancy's. "I can see!" she squealed. "I . . . can . . . see!"

Tiny Doe turned and gazed into the crowd, yet still could not see the faces of her friends, for she had never seen them before to recognize them.

Everyone seemed to understand.

Several children rushed to their feet and came and stood around Tiny Doe, all saying their name.

"This is the first time my daughter has ever been able to put a face with a voice," Morning Flower said, choked with emotion as she stood now with Running Fox and Nancy, while they watched the wonder of the children, who were laughing and touching and hugging excitedly.

Nancy wiped tears from her eyes, for never had she seen such a sweet and wonderful scene. The children still laughed and talked, and Tiny Doe sometimes ran a hand over one face, then another.

"It is a good thing that you have done," Running Fox said, reaching over and hugging Nancy. "I am so proud of you."

"*Ay-uh*, it is a good thing," Morning Flower said, hugging Nancy as Running Fox stepped away.

Everyone was so caught up in what was happening in the council house—that no one was aware of thunder outside, or of the lightning that cracked and zigzagged in lurid flashes across the sky as a storm swept quickly into the village.

The wind suddenly howled, causing the sides of the council house to flap and sway eerily, as though it would collapse at any moment from the torrential rain. The heavy thud of hailstones pounded against the buckskin fabric of the council house.

Some hailstones even came through the smoke hole overhead, for no one had had a chance to close the flap yet. The storm had come so suddenly.

Pandemonium broke out as everyone rushed toward the entranceway.

"I must go and fasten down my own lodge!" Running Fox shouted over the loud rumble of thunder and wind.

Nancy followed him, protecting her eyeglasses with her hands as she ran through the torrential rain, wind, and hail.

Nancy braved the cold raindrops and stinging hailstones to help Running Fox pound the picket pins securely into the ground so that the buckskin-hide tepee would stand strong in the continuing ferocious winds.

More than once Nancy had to readjust her eyeglasses as they slid about on her wet nose. Then, as she took an awkward step toward the entrance flap, she slipped in the mud, fell back, and hit her head hard on a large stone that jutted up from the ground.

Her eyeglasses flew off her face, shattering into a thousand pieces.

Her scream alerted Running Fox that something had happened.

He turned and peered through the drenching rain and pounding hail, stunned when he saw Nancy lying in a pool of muddy water and her eyeglasses not that far from her, destroyed.

He panicked when he saw just how lifeless she looked and he realized that her fall had rendered her unconscious.

Then when he saw blood gushing from a wound at the side of her head, spreading into the water around her, Running Fox ran to her, lifted her gently, and carried her inside his tepee.

As water dripped from his long locks of hair onto Nancy's already wet face, Running Fox carried her to their bed of blankets and pelts and laid her there.

He looked over his shoulder when he heard a voice from that direction.

It was Soft Star saying that she had seen what had happened and she wanted to help in any way that she could.

Running Fox hurried to the flap and held it aside for Soft Star, who was soaked through and through, her rain-soaked black braid lying heavy on her back.

Soft Star knelt beside Nancy.

"She is so pale," Soft Star said, her voice breaking with emotion, for she liked Nancy a great deal. She reached a gentle hand to where the blood still ran, although more lightly now, from Nancy's head wound. "The injury—is it bad?"

"I cannot tell," Running Fox said. "Go for our shaman. Tell Medicine Bear my woman's condition."

Soft Star nodded and hurriedly left. She soon returned with Medicine Bear, then withdrew, giving the shaman and her chief full privacy.

"I shall wait outside while you minister to my woman," Running Fox said.

Running Fox saw the questioning look in his shaman's eyes over the words "my woman," but he ignored it. The only thing that was important now was seeing to Nancy's wound. "I shall be outside as you work your magic," he repeated huskily.

Medicine Bear nodded and opened his large parfleche bag.

Although the rain and hail had stopped, there was still much play of lightning in the heavens overhead, followed by slow rumbles of thunder.

Running Fox picked up a stick, bent low, and drew the figure of a turtle in the wet earth. He prayed to it for better weather and for the storm to go far, far away, for it had caused his woman much distress.

He also gazed heavenward and prayed to the Great Spirit to make his woman well again.

Then he remembered her eyeglasses.

He saw them now where they had landed, not that far from the rock that had caused his woman's injury.

The glass part of the eyeglasses lay in many splintered pieces in the mud.

He gently collected them and wrapped them in a small piece of buckskin, then very carefully picked up the twisted frames, surely too bent ever to wear again even if the lenses had stayed intact.

He turned just as Medicine Bear walked out of his tepee.

He stood quickly and went to his shaman. "How is she now?" he asked urgently.

"She will recover," was all that Medicine Bear

said. Then he walked away, his long gray hair dragging on the rain-soaked ground behind him, his parfleche bag carried at his right side.

"She will recover," Running Fox whispered to himself. The words were like music to his heart.

Chapter 17

The storm had passed. The sky was now clear and a lovely azure blue as Running Fox gazed up at it through his smoke hole.

Then he looked at Nancy, as she still lay in a deep sleep.

When she moaned softly, then slightly turned her head, Running Fox's heart skipped a beat. It seemed she was about to awaken.

But again she lay quiet and still, her eyes closed. Not far away from where she lay were her broken eyeglasses.

Running Fox examined the twisted frames and broken glass.

Only now did he think about what having broken them would mean to Nancy. She had generously given her other pair to the child, which meant that she herself no longer had a way to see.

He glanced toward the closed entrance flap.

Should he go to the child's mother and tell her the dilemma?

No.

He could not do that.

He would never forget the joy, the wonder, in Tiny Doe's eyes, when she had realized that she could see—truly see—for the first time in her life.

Running Fox would not take that away from her, nor would Nancy want him to. She had enjoyed giving of herself to the child and seeing the joy that her gift had brought into the child's heart and life.

Knowing Nancy so well now, Running Fox knew that she would go around half blind herself before taking back the gift of sight that she had given to Tiny Doe.

"What shall we do?" he whispered to himself, again gazing lovingly at Nancy.

Of course, there was only one thing they could do—after she was well enough. They would have to meet with Doc Harris again, for he had said that he would always have spare eyeglasses for Nancy.

But Running Fox knew that each time he wandered far from his village with Nancy the risk of being caught with her was strengthened considerably.

If her stepfather saw her with Running Fox, or if

any white man who would have heard of her disappearance saw her with a red man, Running Fox would not only be placing himself in danger for having abducted her, but his people, as a whole would suffer.

"Running Fox!" Nancy gasped, reaching out toward him. "Running Fox, sit down beside me so that I can touch you."

Running Fox did as she asked, then noticed something different in the way she looked at him now—different from the way she usually looked at him when she was not wearing her eyeglasses.

Nancy swallowed back a sob of joy as she ran her fingers slowly over his face, stunned almost speechless that she could actually see his features clearly—and she didn't have her eyeglasses on!

"I can see," she exclaimed, taking one of his hands and gripping it hard. "Running Fox, what happened? I can see you—not only your shadow—and I don't have my eyeglasses on."

Then pain shot through her head.

She reached up and felt the lump on the side of her head. Her fingers came away covered in a slick, sticky substance.

"I'm injured," she said, seeing how stunned Running Fox was about what she had said only moments ago. "How? And what happened that made me able to see without my eyeglasses?"

Running Fox took both of her hands and held them.

He smiled into her eyes, so glad that a miracle had happened today. Although she had had a bad fall, something positive had come from it.

"During the storm you were helping me to secure my tepee so that the wind would not sweep it away, and you slid and fell," he explained. "You hit your head on a rock. It immediately rendered you unconscious. During the fall, your eyeglasses were also broken. But now you say that you can see without them?"

"Everything," Nancy said, moving to a sitting position. She again slowly ran her fingers over his face, lingering on his lips. "Everything."

She choked back another sob of joy. "For the very first time in my life that I can remember, I can see things without the aid of eyeglasses.

"The blow to my head must have caused it," she said. "The jarring, or something mysterious, must have done it. But no matter, the fact is that I will no longer have to wear eyeglasses. I am in a sense free, totally free, for the first time in my life. I have you, and now I have my eyesight. I could never ask for more than that."

"The Great Spirit works in mysterious ways," Running Fox said, reaching a hand to her face and gently touching her cheek. "And it is good not only that you can see but that you are awake and in control of your faculties. For a while I thought that the blow to the head had done you terrible harm. You slept for so long."

"What is that on the lump on my head?" she asked, again touching it.

"Medicine Bear came and medicated it and prayed over you," Running Fox said. "He is a man of many miracles. Today he and the Great Spirit have given you back your health, as well as your eyesight."

"My eyeglasses?" she said wonderingly. "You say they were broken?"

He reached behind him for the remnants of her eyeglasses. "These are the remains of them," he said.

She took them into her hand, then smiled broadly and tossed them into the flames of the fire. "Never again will I be forced to wear something to help me see," she murmured, so glad when Running Fox wrapped his arms around her and held her. "I am a whole person for the first time in my life."

Suddenly she flinched, as another sharp pain shot through her head and dizziness quickly followed.

"I am not all that well," she conceded. "I'm dizzy and I'm in pain, but not as bad as earlier. And I can stand any pain that comes with giving me back my eyesight."

"But you had best lie back down and rest," Running Fox said, helping her lie down on the bed of pelts and blankets.

He stretched out beside her and held her hand as she closed her eyes. "Wounds and injuries can heal, but one's spirit is a different matter," he said softly. "If your spirit is hurt, sometimes it can never be well again. One must always pray and guard against such hurts as that."

"My spirit is fine," Nancy responded. "But that is only because of you. Had I been forced to live that other life for much longer, I'm almost positive my spirit would have been broken, then died."

"*Ay-uh*, your spirit is fine," Running Fox said, smiling into her eyes.

"Will you tell me things of your people as I lie here and listen?" Nancy asked weakly. "Your voice soothes my inner soul so much. And I do want to know everything that I can so that I will never disappoint you once I become your wife."

"You could never disappoint me," Running Fox said, bringing her hand to his lips and kissing it.

Then he only held it again. "Let me see," he said, considering. "What shall I tell you first? I shall begin by explaining my people's religion to you. The religion of the Lakota consists principally, but not wholly, in the worship of visible things of this world, animate and inanimate. We know of a god and a devil. We call the god Wakantanka, which to us is our Great Spirit. The devil is called Wakan-shicha, the evil spirit."

"We worship God in order to keep the devil from our lives and hearts," Nancy said. "I have never seen my stepfather pick up, much less read, a Bible. That is why his life is guided by evil—by the devil."

"Our people's chief object of worship is Unkteri, the mammoth. We have pieces of the bones of the mammoth in our possession," Running Fox continued.

Nancy was in awe of this and listened intently as he told her more about it. His soothing voice helped her get her mind off the ache of her head.

"The species of mammoth that we worship resembles the buffalo or ox but is of more enormous size than those that wander the earth today. Since it so much exceeded other animals in size, it was only natural that we Lakota adopted it as our chief god. To his worship, our most solemn religious festivals are dedicated."

"Where are those bones found?" Nancy asked, her eyes slowly drifting closed as sleep tried to claim her.

"Even I have found fossil bones, as a young brave," he replied. "I found them at the bottom of a river when I went there during water challenges. The bones were lodged hard in the mud and rock at the river bottom, so I held on to them to keep me down so that I would win the challenge of who could stay beneath the water the longest. As the sun's rays poured through the water onto the huge bones, I realized what they were."

He saw that she was asleep again and knew that it was best that she did have more rest, but he continued telling his tale just in case she might be able to hear him.

"It took many warriors at one time to lift those skeletal remains from the water," he said. "Those bones are highly prized for magical powers."

His Lakota people concluded that Unkteri's dwellings were in the water.

His people's young braves dove often, trying to find more skeletal remains, but no others had been found since that one discovery of Running Fox's long ago.

Because he had been the one to discover them, his people had placed him, even at that young age, at a higher standing than others his age.

It had not been hard for him to be named chief once he was of age!

"Running Fox . . ."

Nancy's calling his name during her sleep made him smile and know that even when she slept he was still very much with her.

As he lay on his back beside his loved one, he gazed heavenward through the smoke hole and said a quiet thank-you to the one high above who looked down at him at all times with His guidance!

Chapter 18

The day was warm, the sun brilliant overhead. The sky was blue, with only an occasional puff of white clouds drifting along the horizon.

Feeling she was truly alive for the first time in her life, her fall now several days behind her, Nancy could hardly believe that she was a short distance from Running Fox's village, being taught how to shoot a rifle.

Running Fox had told her that it was important that she know how to defend herself, for one never knew when the enemy, white- or red-skinned, was planning an attack.

She prayed every night that her stepfather wouldn't come to the village again with his whiskey. If he caught one glimpse of her there, she had no idea what he would do.

Surely he would go to the law and tell them where she was, and that could start a downhill spiral of luck for Running Fox and his people.

"Running Fox, what are you planning to do about my stepfather? Even though I am not there, it doesn't seem to have hampered him," Nancy mused while holding the rifle steady as Running Fox held on to the barrel, helping her.

He replied, his eyes heavy with concern, "It is my plan to find a way to steal and destroy your stepfather's liquor supply. If that does not teach the man a lesson, he will then have to be abducted."

"What?" Nancy gasped, almost dropping the rifle. "You would abduct him?"

"Only if it becomes necessary," Running Fox said. "Shoot the rifle again. It is important to learn how to defend yourself in case there is danger."

"Do you expect that to happen?" Nancy asked, blanching at the thought.

"The red man never knows what to expect next from the white man," Running Fox said. He nodded toward the rifle. "Fire. Aim at the log that I have set up for your target practice and shoot at it."

She stood stiffly and pulled the trigger. She felt like doing a dance when she saw the log flip sideways as the bullet made contact.

"I did it!" she cried, turning wide-eyed toward Running Fox. "I finally hit it!"

Running Fox smiled and eased the rifle from her

hands. "*Ay-uh*, yes, you did," he said. "I am proud of you. You are an astute student. That is enough for today."

Although proud of having finally hit the target, Nancy felt her success somewhat marred by what Running Fox had said a moment ago about finding her stepfather's liquor supply and destroying it.

She knew the danger in that, for where her stepfather stored his whiskey was not that far from Dry Gulch.

"Are you certain you want to destroy the whiskey?" she asked as Running Fox slid his rifle into the gun boot on his steed's right side.

"I must," Running Fox said. "That seems the only way to stop the whiskey runs, at least until the man builds up another supply of the spirit water."

"And he will, you know," Nancy said sadly. "He is a very determined man about this."

"And I am as determined to stop him," Running Fox said, leading Nancy to her horse and helping her into the saddle.

Nancy wanted to do everything within her power to help Running Fox bring her stepfather down.

She would have to forget the danger in order to help him succeed.

"I know exactly where my stepfather stores his whiskey supply," she blurted out, causing Running

Fox to look quickly at her and fork an eyebrow. "I can lead you there."

Running Fox stared at her for a moment longer, then sidled his horse closer to hers. "There will be much danger in going there," he said. "I would not want you to go there with me. You can tell me where it is and I will go with many warriors and destroy it."

"I'm afraid you might not find the right house," Nancy said, swallowing hard. "If you didn't, others might pay for the sins of my stepfather. Please let me go to assure that you do find the right place. I would even enjoy helping you destroy the sinful stuff."

"I have promised to keep you safe, not lead you into the face of danger," Running Fox said, reaching over and gently touching her face. "My *mitawin*, this will be very dangerous."

"I know, but I still want to go," Nancy said. "Running Fox, should you get caught, I want to be there to speak in your behalf."

"Usually words do not come before shooting when it comes to whites' finding the red man in the act of something whites see as illegal," Running Fox said tightly.

"The odds would be against you in all respects if I do not come with you," Nancy said, lifting her chin stubbornly. "I know the exact house. We could destroy the whiskey and hurry away into the darkness before anyone would even realize we were there."

"You are a brave woman to want to do this," Running Fox said, dropping his hand slowly away from her.

"We will go together," he assured her, drawing a quick, sweet smile from her.

"I won't disappoint you," she said, riding beside him as they headed again toward his village.

"You could never disappoint," Running Fox said, truly in awe of this woman in so many ways. When he had taken her from her bed that night, he had never thought to have found his true love, nor a woman with such courage and heart—his companion for life.

He could have been no more proud if she were a warrior who had achieved a goal that brought much praise his way from the Lakota people!

Chapter 19

Carole ran sobbing from the stage of the Crystal Palace. She cringed when she heard the men continuing to chant *"Naughty Carole . . . Naughty Carole!"*

Now she understood why Nancy had despised performing before such an audience. The men were mainly drunkards who saw all women as animals.

Crying harder, she lifted the skirt of her lovely gown and rushed into her dressing room, stopping abruptly when she found Joseph there, standing with his arms folded across his chest, his eyes filled with anger.

"You're worse than your daughter, whore," Joe snapped, stepping up to Carole. He gripped her shoulders hard and gave her a shake. "Stop it. You have another performance. You can't go out there whimpering and with a red face. What do you want to do? Embarrass me?"

"Embarrass?" Carole cried. She yanked herself free of his grip. "I am the one who is embarrassed. Listen to those horrible men. I feel degraded. I feel like a piece of meat. I—I—can't go out there again, Joe. I won't."

He struck her across her face, causing her to fall clumsily against the wall. "You'll do what I say," he growled. "Do you hear?"

"I just can't," Carole said, trembling as she placed a hand on her cheek, which was hot from the blow. "I don't see how Nancy ever did it. I feel dirty and degraded. When I sing for those men, they stare at me as though they are mentally undressing me. My sweet Nancy at least was lucky in one respect. She didn't wear her eyeglasses, so she couldn't see the filthy men. But I can, and I just can't do it anymore, Joe. You'll have to kill me."

"Don't tempt me," Joe grumbled. He shoved her aside and opened the door. "Your audience needs you. Get out there, whore. And when you're through, you'll accompany me on a whiskey run before it gets dark."

"I draw the line there, Joe," Carole snapped back, stiffly holding her chin high, defying him. "I absolutely won't."

"I'll teach you to disobey," Joseph said, yanking the belt from his breeches. He raised it to hit her.

But she didn't give him the chance.

She ran from the room and onto the stage.

Being in front of the crowd of men was better than being at that madman's mercy.

She only wished she could summon the bravery to leave, as had her Nancy.

Someday, oh, someday, she had to find a way, or die an unmerciful death at the hand of the man she had so wrongly fallen in love with.

Chapter 20

The village as a whole was in a state of shock.

Nancy sat at the back of the council house, looking on as everyone crowded inside, solemn and angry.

Since today's council was a private affair for the Fox Band of Lakota, Nancy had not felt it was right to sit with Running Fox, although he, out of what she knew was courtesy and kindness, had asked this of her.

She knew that this was not the time for his people to look to their chief for counsel and leadership and see a white woman at his side.

She wanted to be there, to be a part of the council, since she was going to be their chief's wife, but she did not want to draw any undue attention to herself at such a time as this.

There had been a drunken fight between some young Lakota and Chippewa braves. The Chippewa had traded the Lakota youths spirit water for their prized bows and arrows.

A scuffle had broken out between the youths on a butte. One of the Lakota braves had died when he tripped and fell from the bluff.

That morning at dawn a brave had delivered the news to Running Fox. When he heard the news, his handsome face had drained of color. When Nancy approached him, trying to offer comfort, he had gathered her into his arms.

Clinging to her, he had told her that he had been afraid that something like this would happen. The young braves were obviously drawn to the evil of the spirit water and found ways to indulge behind their parents' and their chief's backs.

The lure of it had been too strong once again.

Now one of their own young braves had died because of it! And even worse, the deed had been done by one of the Lakota's most ardent enemies— the Chippewa.

But just as Running Fox said that he had no choice now but to retaliate, a voice had spoken from outside his entrance flap, a voice that had brought news from the Chippewa camp.

Wind Eagle had been standing sentry when he had spied a Chippewa canoe coming to the shore of the Lakota.

In it was a Chippewa warrior who had been dispatched by his chief, Winter Moon, to convey his condolences for the death of the young brave. Chief Winter Moon had also agreed to a meeting between chiefs in order to settle the matter of their youths' being destroyed by spirit water.

Running Fox had called this council in order to tell his people about this message, and his response to it.

He stood now, courageous and tall, his body sheathed in fringed buckskin, his one lone eagle feather hanging from a lock of hair at the back of his head.

He had painted a stripe of black beneath each of his eyes as his way of showing his remorse over the loss of one of their people's youths.

His eyes reflected the hurt and pain that he felt. He raised a hand and said a prayer to the Great One above, then faced the assembly.

"My people, you know me as a chief who believes in peaceful measures when there is trouble. I have agreed to meet with Chief Winter Moon of the Yellow Feather band of Chippewa to find ways to stop once and for all this thing that has torn asunder too many lives," he said gravely. "I see this meeting as a positive solution. My people, I have put my deeply felt need for vengeance aside and have sent word back to Chief Winter Moon that, yes, there can be a council, but only if it is held at our village."

Gasps of horror rippled through the crowd.

"I see disbelief in some of your eyes, and I understand your feelings," Running Fox said. "The Chippewa have been our *toka*, enemy, since the beginning of time, but now there is someone who is worse still, and that is a man with white skin and a dark heart. This man is an enemy to both the Lakota and the Chippewa. A young man awaits burial rites even now because of a white man—the whiskey peddler. He must be stopped."

One warrior stood—the father of the youth who had died that morning. "My chief, I am one among those who cannot agree to the meeting between you and the Chippewa chief," he said, his voice raw with grief. "I am afraid that it might be a plan to entice you into such a meeting only to kill you. How can you trust a man who until now has been nothing but a thorn in our sides?"

"Trust must be earned, that is true," Running Fox said. He looked directly into the eyes of the grieving father.

He then moved his eyes to the woman who grieved as well.

The mother.

He gazed intently into her red and swollen eyes and saw the pain that he felt even though the brave was not born of his flesh.

He shifted his eyes again and gazed directly into Wind Eagle's. "My warrior, I do understand the pain you are feeling and I ache inside for you. But you do not have to be afraid of your chief being lured into the Chippewa camp. As I said, I have agreed to a meeting only if Chief Winter Moon will come to our village for the special council. I await his response even now. If the Chippewa chief is sincere, we should receive his word of agreement anytime now. If he agrees to meet with me on our own soil, he is to send word back immediately by way of our scout Gray Raven."

"But to meet face-to-face with this chief we all loathe—can you truly say that you will be able to talk in a civil tongue to him?" Wind Eagle asked, his voice breaking. "If I am to be a part of the council, I would not be able to hold back the words that my heart is filled with at this moment."

"And I understand," Running Fox said, nodding. "That is why the council will be between me and the Chippewa chief. After our private meeting, I will be able to determine if he is truly sincere. Then we will meet with all of you in our council house."

Footsteps hurried toward the council house. A moment later Gray Raven stepped inside, his eyes meeting Running Fox's.

"He agreed," Gray Raven said. "The date will be

sent by one of his couriers. If you agree to that date, I personally will go and carry your message to him."

"That is good," Running Fox said, nodding. "Thank you, Gray Raven, for going with such speed to and from the Chippewa village. We can now proceed with the burial rites for our fallen brave."

He gazed at Fast Deer's mother and father. "We will wait until dark to take your fallen son to Ghost Island," he said softly.

He paused, nodded at Nancy, then gazed at his people again. "For now, all whites but one will be ignorant of the grief that has been brought into our village. That one is Nancy. You must understand that she had no role in what happened today, or any other day, as far as the spirit water is concerned. You all know now that she was forced to do what she sorely hated doing. That is one reason she does not leave and return to that world now that she is free to leave."

He knew that they understood that there was another reason why she would not be leaving—she was their chief's *mitawin*.

Nancy felt a blush heat her cheeks, yet she understood why Running Fox had felt the need to say what he had.

"We will disband now from this council house and go to the one that has been raised for the sole purpose of mourning Fast Deer," Running Fox instructed.

"Go now. Each of you say your prayers over Fast Deer's body. When night falls, we will complete the burial services at Ghost Island."

Everyone was glum and silent as the group left the council house.

Nancy stayed behind.

When she and Running Fox were finally alone, they met midway in the large room and embraced.

"It is all so sad," she mused. "I wish that I could do something to help, but I know that the only thing that I can do is be silent."

"After tonight, the full focus of my people will be to find a way to finally stop your stepfather," Running Fox said resolutely. He gently framed her face between his hands. "He has not heeded any warnings. Now he will pay for it."

"You are going to destroy his liquor supply," Nancy said. "When will you do it?"

"Everything must wait until my meeting with Chief Winter Moon is over. Then the man responsible for all of this sadness will pity the day he was born into this world."

Chapter 21

Night had fallen.

The moon was covered by dark clouds, and a low fog hung over the convoy of canoes as they made their way to Ghost Island, their torches lighting the path.

Nancy was in the lead canoe with Running Fox. One of his warriors sat at the far back, holding their torch.

Nancy leaned toward Running Fox. "I'm no longer afraid," she said, wanting to reassure him.

"I knew that you wouldn't be," Running Fox said as he continued to paddle. "That is because you are intelligent and understanding—and you are my *mitawin*."

"I am so proud to be your woman," Nancy said,

reaching a hand to his shoulder and gently touching it. "I am so proud of you."

She tried to see the island, but the fog was too dense to see anything beyond Running Fox.

She waited until he had the canoe beached, then felt his strong arms lift her from the canoe.

The warrior carried their torch and stood beside Nancy as the other canoes came, one by one, the last one carrying the fallen young brave, who was wrapped in blankets.

Beneath the light of the torches, Nancy gasped when she saw Fast Deer's mother for the first time tonight. To show her mourning, her hair was disheveled. She was pale, and her arms were bleeding, having been slashed with a knife.

Just before Fast Deer was taken from the canoe, their people's shaman came up to Fast Deer's mother, took a handful of sage from a small bag, held it above her head, and sprinkled her with it.

"With this I purify you," he said. "I pray that you might begin a new and happier life."

With that, the grieving mother drew her blanket tightly around her and stepped closer to her husband's side.

Low chants filled the air as the young man's body was taken from the canoe.

Nancy stifled a sob as Fast Deer was carried past her, the Lakota people falling into step behind him as the procession moved slowly toward the burial ground.

Running Fox took Nancy gently by an elbow and led her through the trees, the torches' flares waving and swaying in the soft breeze.

Finally they came to the burial ground. One of the braves had come ahead of them and prepared a scaffold.

Soon the body lay atop the scaffold; it would remain there for a few days until the burial.

Nancy sat with Running Fox during the ceremony. The shaman prayed and chanted, and then presented a lock of Fast Deer's hair wrapped in cloth to his mother, who would hang it in her lodge beside the spear his father had been making for him.

After the ceremony was completed, all but Fast Deer's family departed again in the canoes, returning to their main camp.

"Later, when Fast Deer is buried, his family will come often and sit with him, as they would have gone to the fireside of their departed one," Running Fox explained as Nancy anxiously waited for their canoe to arrive at the other side of the lake, away from the island. "As it is, Fast Deer's soul has already departed to the land of the ghosts."

Chapter 22

Nancy could hardly believe that she was actually attending an important meeting between two powerful Indian chiefs—Running Fox and Winter Moon, the middle-aged chief of the Yellow Feather Band of the Chippewa tribe.

Nancy had felt uncomfortable at first when the older chief had discovered her in Running Fox's tepee, especially since he had seen her so often with the whiskey peddler. The older chief considered her just as guilty as the whiskey peddler in his enterprise to corrupt the Chippewa braves.

Running Fox tried to explain that Nancy no longer rode with the whiskey man, and that, in fact, the Lakota were protecting her from the evil man. Even when he told Chief Winter Moon that Nancy was attending the meeting because she had valuable information about where her stepfather kept the whiskey, the older chief ignored her presence.

Nancy had to wonder why the suspicious chief had even agreed to this meeting, especially away from the security of his own village. She hoped that Running Fox's preparations had made an impression on him.

The fresh aroma of paint still hung in the air. She gazed over the entranceway, smiling as she recalled how, just before the older chief's arrival, she had watched Running Fox paint a picture over his entranceway, on the inside of his tepee. He had painted a pipe in red and yellow, which denoted the pipe that he was going to award to the older chief. Directly opposite this, at the back of his lodge, he had painted an image of the rising sun.

He had explained to her that these paintings were symbols of welcome and goodwill to men under the bright sun, all of which was meant to prove to Chief Winter Moon Running Fox's sincerity in wanting them to come together as allies.

She knew that the time had almost arrived for Running Fox to award the older chief the pipe. Covertly, she studied Chief Winter Moon. From his piercing gaze and the firm expression of his mouth, she knew he was accustomed to command, and he had a natural dignity of manner while conducting business with Running Fox.

A moment later her attention was drawn back to

Running Fox. She watched breathlessly as he slowly unwrapped the large pipe of polished stone that he had finished painting only last evening for presentation to Winter Moon.

She watched the older chief's eyes, hoping for some sign of appreciation. Up to now, there had been only a stern sort of coldness.

"With this pipe, I hope to seal all wounds made by our elders which made enemies of the Lakota, and your people, the Chippewa," Running Fox said. He held the pipe out for Winter Moon. "This pipe was made by my own hands for you. I, myself, took the stone from the bedrock of redstone to make this gift, for the sole purpose of opening a friendship between you, the proud Chippewa chief of the Yellow Feather Band, and I, the proud chief of my Fox Band. Should you accept, it will be a new beginning between our two peoples. Today, there are more whites on land that once solely belonged to us red men. It is important that we red men come together as one against the many white eyes. When you smoke this pipe, as will I, that bond between us, and our peoples, will be sealed. Our hearts will be as one."

Nancy scarcely breathed as she waited for Chief Winter Moon to accept the gift.

She looked slowly over at the older chief. She had found it hard to read this man, for he seemed to keep so much inside himself.

Finally, Winter Moon reached out and very gently took the pipe from Running Fox.

He nodded a silent thank-you, then rested the pipe on his lap as he reached inside a parfleche bag that he had brought with him and took out a small buckskin bag, closed by drawstrings.

Running Fox glanced over at Nancy, smiled, then as quickly looked at what the older chief was doing as Winter Moon unfastened the tiny bag and slowly sprinkled tobacco from his personal tobacco stash into the bowl of the pipe.

After seeing the older chief place his tobacco into the bowl of the pipe, knowing that he had truly accepted the gift, as well as the friendship that came with it, and was ready to exchange smokes with Running Fox, Running Fox reached for a small twig at the edge of the fire.

He lit the tip of it, then held it to the tobacco as Winter Moon placed the pipe stem between his lips.

Winter Moon sucked on it for a moment, inhaling the smoke, then let it out through his lips as he handed the pipe to Running Fox to smoke from.

Running Fox first blew four whiffs to the sun, then four to the earth, and passed the pipe back for Winter Moon to do the same.

The pipe was then placed on a stone between Running Fox and Winter Moon. Both men rested their hands on their knees and crossed their legs.

"It is good that you came and accepted the friendship that has been too long in coming between us and our people," Running Fox said gravely. "It is time that we work together for the better of our people."

"*Ay-uh*, yes, that is so," Chief Winter Moon said, nodding. "The recent tragedies that have befallen our youth have opened my people's eyes. It is with a heavy heart that I come today to tell you how sorry my people as a whole are over your young brave's death. My young braves who wronged yours are confined even now away from everyone, until they see the wrong they have done."

"Have you come to a conclusion as to what you feel should be done about the whiskey man?" Running Fox asked, giving Nancy a quick glance, then gazing directly into the older chief's faded eyes again.

"Something has arisen since our exchange of peaceful overtures between us," Winter Moon said slowly.

"And that is?" Running Fox asked, forking an eyebrow.

"Word was brought into my village from one of my most trusted scouts that the whiskey man has heard about the tragedy and has said that he will no longer be offering his spirit water for trade to any red man, young or old. He sent his sincere apologies."

Nancy's eyes widened.

She glanced quickly over at Running Fox for his reaction, and she saw that what Winter Moon said had stunned him speechless.

"He said that he was afraid to send word into your camp, since it was one of your youths who most recently died after partaking of the spirit water," Winter Moon said. "So he asked that I convey his sympathies for him since he had heard about our planned meeting."

"And do you feel that his words are sincere?" Running Fox said, his eyes narrowing angrily. "Can you believe a man such as he who has caused so much pain and heartache among our people with his trade of spirit water?"

"Only time will tell," Winter Moon said nonchalantly. "It is worth waiting to see. Do you not agree? You know as well as I that should we retaliate and harm the white man, the white community would retaliate in their own ugly ways. Many of our people could die. We have already lost enough at the hands of white men. We cannot chance losing anything or anyone else. The land that we can call ours has dwindled now to being only one-third of what it was because of the white eyes cheating us. Should we have to stand up against them and fight, face-to-face, hand to hand, over the white liquor man, we might never again be as strong as we are now. So what say you, Running Fox? Should we wait this man out and see if he tells truth or falsehood and hope none of our youth are tricked again into trading for his firewater? Or do we stop him now and chance what might happen to us as a result?"

Nancy was stunned over the direction this meeting had gone. The older chief was trying hard to hide his fear in order not to lose his dignity, but at the same time he was proving that he was afraid. She was saddened that the white community had caused this once-powerful man to be afraid to stand up for his rights.

She gazed at Running Fox. She knew he was feeling trapped.

She also knew her stepfather was lying. Joe had a huge storage house of whiskey. He would not just let it sit and go to waste.

And he had never made as much money from the sale of his whiskey to the white community as he did from trading for those expensive pelts from the red man.

She could tell that Running Fox didn't believe it any more than she did, yet she knew that he felt it was important to have this camaraderie with the older chief.

"I agree to your plan," Running Fox said, his voice thick with emotion. "But should we discover that the man lied to you, and if he brings spirit water into our midst again, we must not delay any longer in making plans to stop him."

"That is good," Winter Moon said.

Chief Winter Moon lifted the pipe from the stone.

He filled its bowl with more tobacco, but this time he did not light it first himself.

Instead, he handed it to Running Fox.

After Running Fox placed the stem between his lips, Winter Moon lit the tobacco.

As Running Fox smoked from the pipe first, then handed it over to Winter Moon, Nancy was touched by the ceremony, for Running Fox had told her that tobacco was the greatest possession owned by the red man and that when shared it created a lasting bond.

This smoke shared and completed, the pipe was wrapped in the cloth and Winter Moon stood up, holding it to his chest.

"We move now to the council house so that we can share what we have decided with our warriors," Running Fox said. He turned to Nancy. "I will not be long."

She realized that he was telling her that she should not join the meeting where only the warriors would come together.

She nodded and stepped aside to watch the two chiefs leave.

She was worried about their decision because she knew how untrustworthy Joe was. If he had said that he would no longer bring his whiskey among the red community, he was lying.

She wondered just how long it would take for Running Fox and Winter Moon to discover this.

She glanced over at the beautiful white doeskin pelt that Winter Moon had brought to Running Fox as an offering of friendship.

She reached out and touched it, sighing at its softness.

She envisioned herself wearing a dress made of this pelt—perhaps on her wedding day?

Smiling, she gazed up through the smoke hole, and gasped when she saw a beautiful rainbow arching overhead with its wonderful colors.

Just before the older chief's arrival, there had been a storm, which had only recently blown past.

"It's as though it is an omen sent from the heavens, which might be a sign of peace everlasting between these two chiefs and their people," she whispered.

Chapter 23

The day was filled with music, dancing, games, and excitement as two bands of Indians came together as friends after having been enemies for so long.

A veritable feast had been prepared. The Lakota women had made a soup of cooked wild rice, strained and mixed with broth made from choice venison.

Nancy had been told that the women pounded dried venison almost to a flour and kept it in water until the nourishing juices were extracted, then mixed with it some pounded maize that was browned beforehand.

She sat among the crowd, watching games being played by the adults. The children had already almost exhausted themselves beneath the bright rays of the sun.

Her eyes followed Running Fox as he ran toward the lake. He wore only a breechclout, his moccasins having been discarded moments ago.

The Chippewa chief's son, Two Feathers, who was Running Fox's same age, ran toward the water behind him.

Nancy stood up and hurried to the lake's embankment, crowding in among the others who had run there to watch the competition between Running Fox and Two Feathers.

Two days ago, Running Fox had sent out invitations to all of Chief Winter Moon's people to join his Lakota people at his village.

The invitations had been in the form of bundles of tobacco and had been taken to each household at the Chippewa village.

The acceptance to Running Fox's kind invitation had been sent back in the same fashion . . . with bundles of tobacco made from the Chippewa tobacco harvest.

And today was the celebration, the first alliance ever between these two bands.

All day long the tribes had played games and music had filled the air. Among the musical instruments were flutes made of red cedar, drums, and rattles, which were dried gourds filled with seeds.

The music played rhythmically now, as Running

Fox swam even farther from the shore, with Two Feathers not that far from him.

Running Fox had told Nancy earlier about this main challenge of the day between himself and the chief's son, who would himself become chief after Winter Moon passed on to the other side.

He had told her then that even in the winter, when ice formed a thin crust over the lake, spaces would be cut in the ice so that warriors could plunge into the water to see how much cold they could endure, and who could endure it the longest.

But today the water was warm, the sunlight filtering through the surface of the water.

Cheers suddenly erupted as both Running Fox and Two Feathers dove, as though they were following those sun rays.

Nancy covered a slight gasp with a hand, for she knew this was the true challenge of the day. It was a contest of strength and endurance conducted in the water as the divers would search for a rock or the root of a tree to hold on to in order to see who could stay below the surface the longest.

Earlier, Running Fox had actually admitted to her that he was torn about how this particular challenge should end. If it appeared as though he would be the victor, he wondered if he should back off and instead allow his challenger to be the victor in order to strengthen the tenuous bond between the bands.

Nancy's pulse raced as she anxiously watched the water, aware now that the music had stopped and a hush had fallen over the crowd. Some women covered their eyes, almost afraid now to see what the outcome would be. Would the victor bring the other man ashore, unconscious from having forced himself to hold his breath too long?

Suddenly one head broke through the surface of the water, and the crowd gasped aloud. Two Feathers surfaced, and then only a moment later, Running Fox appeared as well. Both of them gasped for breath as they swam to shore, and it was not hard to see their struggle as they stepped from the water.

Their legs were trembling and their bare chests were heaving.

But it was obvious who the victor was.

Running Fox!

Still no one said anything. The crowd only watched as the two water-soaked warriors turned and faced one another.

Nancy clutched her hands tightly at her sides. Then her eyes opened wide when both men began laughing, then hugging, their alliance clearly cemented by the test of time in the water.

"We are both the victor!" Running Fox said, now stepping away from Two Feathers, yet resting his hands on the young Chippewa warrior's shoulders. "I watched you break away from the root of the tree at the same moment as I. If not for that turtle that swam suddenly in my path, I would have surfaced at the same moment as you. I let the turtle pass, then came on to the surface."

Suddenly the silence among the people was broken by loud roars and cheers as they formed a tight circle around the two men.

Nancy stood back with the women, unable to fight back the tears of happiness that suddenly fell from her eyes.

She had truly been afraid for Running Fox.

Her heart skipped a beat when the crowd suddenly parted and he came through the opening toward her.

When he stepped up to her, his long black hair hanging wet and dripping down his magnificently muscled back, his dark eyes smiling into hers, Nancy fully appreciated the special attention he bestowed on her.

"My *mitawin*, did you see?" he asked, searching her eyes. "It was the same as the other time when I found the remains of the mammoth. I found others today. As Two Feathers clung to a root of a tree, I clung to a monstrous bone. It is an omen, *mitawin*, an omen that includes you in my happiness."

Touched deeply by his words, and the way he so openly singled her out at such a time as this, in front of their guests, the Chippewa people, Nancy felt at a loss for words.

But Running Fox ensured that she would not have to do or say anything.

He stepped up beside her and swept an arm around her waist. It was then that everyone, including the Chippewa, knew that he would soon wed this woman!

There weren't as many gasps, or looks of wonder, as Nancy had expected.

But when she glanced over at Chief Winter Moon, she again saw disapproval in his eyes, as she had the day she had stayed in Running Fox's lodge during the private council between the two chiefs.

She wasn't sure how to take this man's obvious dislike of her, especially since it was so important now that the Chippewa and the Lakota become not only close allies but friends as well, in order to combat this thing that had come among them—the spirit water that her stepfather had brought into their lives.

"When the moon is full again in the sky, I will take this woman as my wife, and all are invited to join our celebration of love!" Running Fox said, now directing his gaze at the older chief. "I will not send tobacco invitations to you and your people this time, for I am personally inviting you now to join us on that night of the full moon. Will you come? Will you bring your people with you?"

"*Ay-uh*, I will come. We will come," Winter Moon said, a strange sort of huskiness in his voice as he again turned his full attention to Nancy, causing a strange sort of chill to ride her spine.

"That is good," Running Fox said, nodding. Then he turned back to the crowd and said, "Prepare the plates with food for everyone!" He beamed with happiness and pride over how today's events had proven to be filled with camaraderie between his people and the Chippewa.

Two Feathers joined Running Fox and placed a hand on Running Fox's shoulder. "My friend, it is with a warm heart that I congratulate you on your upcoming nuptials," he said. "I will soon wed, myself."

With a flick of a wrist, Two Feathers beckoned to a lovely young woman. She wore doeskin embellished with colorful beads, and her hair fell in two braids down her back.

Her dark eyes seemed filled with warmth and sunshine, and her smile was soft and sweet as she looked first at Nancy and then at Running Fox.

Two Feathers slid an arm around her waist. "This is Morning Sun," he said proudly. "She is going to be the mother of my children."

Nancy and Running Fox quickly congratulated them. Soon the music began again, and people gathered in small groups, talking and laughing, as they devoured platters of food. Winter Moon, Running Fox and Nancy, and Two Feathers and his soon-to-be bride sat together, enjoying the food and the merriment all around them.

Nancy had been told before today's celebration that much meat of wild game had been put away with great care during the previous autumn in anticipation of such a feast. Wild rice and the choicest of the dried venison had been kept all winter, and freshly dug turnips, ripe berries, and an abundance of fresh meat were also served today.

As a deepening twilight settled over the camp, songs and drumming around the fire began.

By the time the moon replaced the sun in the sky, much food had been eaten, and now various groups were taking turns dancing.

Nancy felt at peace with herself, so glad to be a part of tonight's glorious moments.

She gazed heavenward at the sliver of moon, smiling as she recalled how Running Fox had told everyone that when the moon became full again in the sky he would take Nancy as his wife!

She wished on the stars that those long nights would speed by.

She glanced over her shoulder in the direction of Dry Gulch and wondered how things were faring between her mother and her stepfather. She grimaced at the thought of her mother being onstage at the Crystal Palace, at the mercy of those crazed men who drank too much.

"*Mitawin*, tomorrow I will teach you how to use

a bow and arrow," Running Fox said, drawing her attention to him as Two Feathers and Morning Sun got up and mixed with the dancers, laughing and moving in time with the rhythmic beats of the drums, flutes, and rattles.

Nancy was somewhat stunned that he would think of such a thing at a time like this, and she wondered what she might have missed while Running Fox and Two Feathers had held their heads together, talking more quietly and seriously than they had all day.

She wanted to ask what they had been discussing, but she knew that had he wanted her to know, he would have included her.

"Would you like that?" Running Fox asked, taking her hands. "You did quite well at learning the art of firing the rifle, but the skill of using a bow and arrow can sometimes be harder than aiming correctly in order to shoot a firearm accurately enough."

"The bows seem so big," Nancy said, recalling several bows that she had seen at the back of his lodge, where he stored his weapons.

"There are those made for women that will be the sort that you will use," Running Fox said, smiling.

"I would love to try," Nancy quickly said, then stood with Running Fox.

His eyes gleamed as he gazed into hers. "Do you

want to join the dancers?" he asked, glancing over his shoulder at them.

Nancy gazed at them, too, realizing that the way they were dancing was far distant from the way white people danced. She knew that she wasn't quite ready to try that, especially since there were so many people who would see her clumsiness.

"I would rather take a walk," she murmured.

Running Fox swept an arm around her waist and led her away from the crowd and into the shadows of trees. He turned to her and drew her up next to him.

When their lips met in a soft kiss, she clung to him, so glad to finally be alone with him.

But when someone called his name, Running Fox turned quickly away from Nancy, then smiled down at her. "I am being beckoned," he said softly.

"Go," she said. "I will stay here for a moment longer."

"Are you tired?" he asked, concerned.

"It has been a long day, but, no, I am not as tired as I am eager to retire to your tepee, and I am sure you know why," she said, reaching a hand to his lips, slightly tracing them with a forefinger. "You do, don't you?"

He laughed huskily, kissed her again, then ran into the light of the outdoor fire.

She watched as he mingled with several warriors, both Chippewa and Lakota.

It was a sight to see, for she knew that history was being made there as two warring tribes were now allies!

"I hope it will last," she whispered. "Oh, Lord, should it not . . ."

Chapter 24

Nancy sighed as she looked around her. Time had passed so quickly. It was now a beautiful fall day. "A gopher's last look back," her father used to say about the last warm days of late autumn when he would come in covered by dust after a full day's harvest in the fields.

That afternoon, Running Fox had given Nancy her first lesson with the bow and arrow. She had felt extremely awkward as she tried to manipulate the weapon. She doubted she could ever learn to use it.

She had been glad to relinquish both the bow that was embossed with porcupine quills and the beautifully worked quiver of arrows to Running Fox.

Running Fox now carried them, and Nancy carried the rifle, feeling confident that she could

fire it accurately enough should they run into
trouble.

She smiled over at Running Fox as they continued on a leisurely walk up the path that took them
to a little rock-garden meadow with wildflowers
and murmuring brooks. Beyond lay a wide-open
prairie, where nothing moved but the wind, and
where at the fringes of the meadow last year's dead
pine needles lay atop the mulched-in needles of the
year before.

Nancy studied Running Fox at length. She was
so happy to be with him like this, alone and seemingly without a care in the world. The celebration
between the Lakota and Chippewa had been a success, and Running Fox had a look of satisfaction on
his face as he continued looking straight ahead, always keeping a sharp lookout.

He wore a full outfit of buckskin today, with
both the sleeves of his shirt and the sides of his leggings fringed.

His hair lay long and loose down his back.

He looked so handsome with the bow slung over
his shoulder, the quiver of arrows secured at his
back. A knife dangled from his belt in its handsome
sheath.

They were quite alone, their horses left behind to
feast on the thick grass.

Some time ago she and Running Fox had walked
past a group of women who were busy digging

wild turnips that were growing on the hillsides and plucking chokeberries that were ripe in the thickets along the river.

Running Fox had explained to her how the women dug the turnips. He had said that they carried long, sharp sticks, with which to pry the turnips from the ground. When a bunch of four or five turnips had been gathered, the long white roots were braided together in order to be more easily carried.

They would be taken home and hung in the sun to dry, then put away in rawhide bags, where they would last for a long time. In the winter, dried turnips were put in the meat soup and cooked.

Nancy always paid close attention to what Running Fox said about the women's duties, for she would soon join them, digging the roots and other things for her own home, for her own husband.

And then everything seemed to change in a heartbeat when Running Fox stopped her in midstep.

"What's wrong?" she asked, searching his eyes and then following their path to see what he was staring so hard at. "What are you looking at?"

"A lynx might be near," Running Fox said cautiously, still staring at the hairs on a cottonwood tree not that far from where they were now standing.

"A lynx?" Nancy said nervously, her heart skipping a beat. "How do you know?"

Running Fox pointed to the tree and the grayish brown hairs that hung loosely from the bark. "A lynx performs an ancient feline ritual called 'rubbing,'" he explained in a low voice. His eyes now moved cautiously around them, watching for other signs of the animal. "The cat presses its cheek and neck against a tree, leaving behind a few hairs. We must be very careful now."

"Especially me, a woman who for most of her life had to wear eyeglasses in order to see anything," Nancy said, laughing nervously.

"You were beautiful even when you wore eyeglasses," Running Fox said, trying to keep the atmosphere as light as possible between them, for he now knew for certain that the lynx was near.

He could almost smell it!

"*Hakamya-upo*, come on, but be careful now," he said, walking stealthily onward.

Just as he said that, he saw two sharp-pointed ears peeking just above the surface of some forsythia bushes.

Before he could grab an arrow from his quiver, or even warn Nancy, the lynx made a sudden and desperate leap.

Running Fox tried to dodge, but the animal was too quick for him.

The lynx caught Running Fox on the shoulder with its great paw and knocked him down, then instantly retreated.

Stunned more by the quickness of the animal than by the blow, Running Fox was able to keep his senses about him.

"*Mitawin*, watch out!" he shouted. He rolled out of the way just as the lynx leapt a second time.

Nancy was stunned, so afraid that she felt frozen to the spot, but Running Fox's cry brought her to her senses.

Just as the lynx spotted her, his next prey apparent, Nancy lifted the rifle shakily, aimed between the animal's eyes, and fired.

She cried out and felt ill when blood squirted from the wound as the animal leapt straight up, then fell motionless almost at Nancy's feet. Running Fox now stood beside her, the rifle in his hand ready to fire again should he need to.

But there was no need.

The animal was dead.

Trembling, Nancy turned to Running Fox, her eyes moving quickly over him to see if he had been wounded. "Are—you—all right?" she gulped out, so glad that she didn't see any blood on him other than what had sprayed from the cat's wound onto his clothes and hers.

"The animal gave me quite a blow, but only with the back of its paw," Running Fox said, still staring at the stilled lynx.

He turned to Nancy and gave her a wide smile,

glad that she had been an astute student with the rifle.

"*Ay-uh*, I am fine," he said, smiling. "And, my *mitawin*, you conquered a formidable foe today."

His eyes suddenly twinkled. "All warriors who succeed at doing such a deed as this always give out two good war whoops," he said. "Let me hear yours."

"War whoops?" Nancy said, her eyebrows arching.

Then she laughed softly. "I don't have the breath," she confessed. "My heart is still beating so hard it might even knock out a rib or two."

"Then I shall do the war whoop for you."

He did the war whoops, then drew her gently into his arms and held her until she stopped trembling.

After he had assured himself that she was going to be all right, he stepped away from her and gestured toward the animal.

"Lynx pelt today, bear tomorrow!" he said, giving Nancy a quick smile.

Nancy's eyes widened at that comment, and she visibly shuddered at the thought.

Running Fox laughed softly. "I was only jesting," he said. "There will be no bear hunt tomorrow."

"Thank goodness," Nancy said, feeling as though she had just learned to breathe normally again.

"There was no lynx hunt today, either, but since we were forced into it by the animal, we will gladly take its pelt," Running Fox said.

He lifted the animal by its front paws and dragged it in the direction of their tethered horses.

Although she and Running Fox came out of this ordeal unharmed, Nancy was still trembling inside because of what had just happened. She had seen her father forced into killing wildcats that had feasted on his cows. She knew the cats deserved to die, yet it always saddened her to see an animal killed, especially a beautiful one.

But she knew she must get over that sort of thinking, for the Lakota would have to kill many animals in order to survive. The animals, such as the deer, were used not only for food but also for lodge coverings.

As Running Fox lifted the lynx and placed it on the rear of his horse, she saw just how lovely the pelt was and knew that it would be used to make something beautiful and useful.

Running Fox saw Nancy gazing at the lynx and could almost read her thoughts about the loss of this beautiful animal.

"There is a dance called the Dance of the Lynx," he said, drawing her eyes quickly to him. "Do you want to hear about it?"

"Yes, please tell me," Nancy said, glancing at the

animal again, then gazing into Running Fox's dark eyes.

"There are many dances of my people. The lynx is only one of them," Running Fox said. "The main dancer in charge brings forth a decorated tail of a lynx. He holds it aloft while everyone sings to the accompaniment of rattles and drums. The lone dancer places a stick, painted red, on the ground to represent a tree. He then takes the tail and imitates the movements of a lynx hunting squirrels. First it walks around, and then it sits down and looks up at the tree, as if in pursuit of a squirrel, but each time it returns and sits down. Finally the dancer makes a quick dash for the tree. He carries the tail rapidly up one side and down the other. As the rhythmic drumming and singing continue, the dancer returns the lynx tail back to his bag."

"What happens then?" Nancy asked as the tale came to a sudden end.

"Another dancer is chosen and he goes through his own gestures of whatever he is imitating," Running Fox said.

He smiled and lifted Nancy onto her saddle. "Much has been learned today, not only for the necessity of one's survival but also about dances."

Nancy smiled. "I am in awe of all that we do together, especially of everything that you teach me," she said.

"It is time to go home now," Running Fox

said, mounting his steed, the lynx on the horse behind him.

They headed back in the direction of his village.

Running Fox looked over at Nancy. "I am so proud of you," he said thickly. "And the rest of my people will also be as proud. They will see you now as not only lovely but truly valuable to the survival of our people. They will see you as someone brave and worthy of being called Lakota woman."

"Lakota woman?" Nancy said, marveling at it.

"Yes, my Lakota woman," Running Fox said with a nod.

Chapter 25

The fire's glow cast its light on Nancy's face as Running Fox lay over her, blanketing her with his body.

He gazed down at her with adoration in his midnight-dark eyes. "My Lakota woman, you have never looked more radiant than now," he said, brushing a soft tendril of hair back from her eyes. "There is such a peaceful calm about you."

"That is because I am so happy with my life, a life that now includes you," Nancy murmured.

The way he was looking at her created a small flutter deep in her belly.

She sucked in a wild breath of rapture when she felt him thrust his manhood inside her, then begin his slow, rhythmic strokes.

Sighing, she twined her arms around his neck

and closed her eyes as her body grew feverish with the need of what his body was promising her.

He pressed his lips softly against hers and kissed her with an easy sureness, then buried his face next to her neck as he moved slowly and deliberately within her.

He ran a hand across her narrow waist, her full hips. Then he cradled her close as the euphoria that filled his entire being became almost more than he could bear.

His whole body throbbed with the intensity of his feelings for her.

His steel arms enfolded her as he moved more eagerly in her, as what seemed like white-hot flames roared in his ears.

Holding her face now between his palms, he caressed her with his gaze.

"Please kiss me," she whispered, her cheeks hot with her need. "Oh, do you not feel how I want—how I need you?"

"*Ay-uh*, I feel it all," Running Fox said, gazing down at her with his passion-clouded eyes.

He bent his head to her lips and kissed her again, the frantic need for her causing him to speed up his strokes, deeper and deeper within her.

"I feel so much," Nancy whispered. "It is all beautiful. I have never felt so alive!"

His mouth closed hard upon hers again as he molded her closer to the contours of his body, then made one last deep thrust that sent them both spiraling into bliss, their bodies quivering and quaking, and then stilled as they now only clung together, each breathing against the other's cheek.

Nancy felt herself slowly descend from her cloud of rapture. "Each time I feel so much more," she said as he moved away from her, then rolled over onto his back beside her.

"That is the way it should be," Running Fox said, taking one of her hands in his. "It is so good to have you."

"And I'm not going anywhere, ever," Nancy said softly.

"You promise?" Running Fox said, smiling as he leaned up on an elbow so that they could look into one another's eyes.

"With every beat of my heart. For always." She giggled. "A cross-my-heart-and-hope-to-die promise."

"A what sort of promise?" Running Fox said, arching an eyebrow.

She explained the expression to Running Fox.

He scooted next to her and held her endearingly close. "You saved my life today," he said. "Thank you."

"As you saved mine that night you came into my room and took me away from my misery," Nancy said, swallowing hard. "I can never thank you enough for that."

"I am glad that you are thanking me, not cursing me for having disturbed your sleep," he said, chuckling.

"You can disturb my sleep anytime you wish," Nancy said happily.

He swept his arms around her and kissed her again with lips of fire, stealing her breath away as passion rose again between them.

Chapter 26

Everything that had been so wonderful for Nancy was instantly shattered when one of Running Fox's scouts came to him and told him that her mother was missing.

Rumor had it that she had been abducted.

Guilt stabbed at Nancy's heart for having left her mother at the mercy of Joe, yet had Nancy even tried to rescue her, she knew that her mother wouldn't have gone with her. Her mother might despise Joe now for what he had forced on her, yet the man seemed to have some strange sort of hold over her.

"Running Fox, who would do such a thing—and why?" Nancy said as the scout rode away.

"You have told me the sort of men who frequent your stepfather's establishment, so perhaps one of those whiskey-crazed men did it," he said. He drew her into his embrace. "I am sorry about your *ina*."

"I feel so guilty for having turned my back on her," Nancy said, suddenly sobbing. "But there was nothing I could do. She wouldn't have left even had I gone back and tried to talk her into it. I believe she was afraid of losing the security that Joe gave her, strange as it was."

Then a thought struck her that made her step quickly away from Running Fox. Her eyes were wide as she wiped the last of the tears from them. "Now that both I and my mother have come up missing, will the white authorities suspect that your warriors did it? It is no secret how the Lakota feel about my stepfather. What if the law believes you gave the orders to abduct me first, and then my mother, to avenge what my stepfather caused among the Lakota youth by trading his whiskey for their pelts?"

"I must get you safely to Ghost Island," Running Fox said decisively. "If what you say is true, that the white authorities do suspect my people of having a role in both disappearances, they will more than likely come soon to investigate."

"No," Nancy said, stubbornly lifting her chin. "I can't go there and hide while my mother is out there somewhere at the mercy of some madman."

Then the color drained from her face. "Or she might have been taken by Chief Winter Moon's warriors," she said, her voice drawn. "I'll never forget how the chief kept looking at me. I thought it was because he resented my presence among those who came with him for the celebration. But what if it was because he was forming a plan to abduct a white woman for his own act of vengeance against my stepfather? Perhaps seeing me made him think of my mother, someone who was special to my stepfather, too. What if he sent his warriors to abduct her? What if she is there even now at the chief's village? She would never be treated as kindly as you and your people have treated me. Yes, you and I fell in love, whereas she is a woman married to a man everyone despises. If Chief Winter Moon does have her, what might happen to her?"

"I do not see any of that as a possibility," Running Fox said, placing a gentle hand on her cheek. "*Ay-uh*, I saw resentment in the older chief's eyes when he looked at you, because he found it hard to understand how I could have fallen in love with you, a white woman. Although he was my *toka*, enemy, for so long, he is no less a man of his word. He suggested we wait to see if the whiskey peddler spoke truth when he said he would not come among his or my people again with his spirit water. Surely it would not be he who would go against his own suggestions and abduct the white woman."

"Then what do you think has happened to her?"

Nancy said, tears streaming from her eyes once again.

"We will search for answers," Running Fox said, gently drawing her into his embrace. "My warriors and I, not you. I still feel it is important to take you to Ghost Island, where no one but my people will see you."

Nancy stepped away from him. "I can't go there," she said. "I must be able to go with you as you search for answers about my mother's disappearance. I no longer look like Naughty Nancy who performed onstage at the Crystal Palace. I look like a Lakota woman now."

She reached behind her and touched the long braid that hung down her back, and then ran a hand down the front of her doeskin dress.

"Running Fox, please say that I can go with you. I even know how to ride a horse now. I can shoot a rifle well enough to protect myself. I am capable in every way to ride with you and your warriors as you seek answers about my mother's disappearance."

She sighed heavily and looked in the direction of Dry Gulch. "I believe my stepfather is somehow responsible for my mother being gone," she said, her voice breaking. She gazed into Running Fox's eyes again. "If my mother wasn't cooperating with him, not doing everything he ordered her to do, he might have done something rash. If she balked at replacing me onstage so that the drunken, filthy men could ogle and berate her, I truly believe my stepfather would get rid of her and find someone else to take both our places in his life."

She wiped tears from her eyes. "Joe might have become tired of my mother if she worried constantly about my welfare," she said solemnly. "I should have found a way to let her know that I was all right, yet had I done that, she would have told Joe and he would have come for me with much help from the law. I just couldn't chance that."

Seeing Nancy's torment and knowing that he would have to tie her up to keep her from joining him on the search, Running Fox took her hand and walked with her from his lodge.

He stood in the center of the village and shouted out orders for his men to meet for a quick council.

Running Fox relayed the news. He understood their looks of uncaring about the situation, and he saw the tightening of their jaws when they realized what their chief was asking of them. He was asking them to join a search for the lost woman, a woman who was married to the very man they all loathed.

"I understand why you would not want to join a hunt for someone you have no fond feelings for, but we are talking about my woman's mother," Running Fox said. He looked from man to man. "You know what your mothers are to you, do you not? My woman has the feelings of a daughter for a mother. She is distraught over what might have happened to her. I have promised her that I will search for her mother. I need several of you to join the search."

There was a strained silence, then one by one, the warriors stepped forward, until all of them stood ready to help their chief, even though the resentment they felt for the woman they would be searching for was still in their eyes.

"My *mitawin* will join us," Running Fox said, causing the men to step quickly back to where they had originally been standing.

Running Fox glared from one to the other. "You change your mind so quickly?" he growled. "Which of you will change your mind again and step forth to join me on the search? It is your chief asking this of you. Who among you defies your chief in such a way?"

Nancy scarcely breathed as she looked from warrior to warrior, some gazing intensely back at her with the same kind of bitterness she had seen upon first arriving at the village.

She looked over at Running Fox. She was ready to tell him that perhaps he should call off the search, for she did not want to be the cause of his men showing such disdain toward him.

But before she said anything, all of the warriors who had stepped forward before stepped forward again.

"And so you are ready to join the search, I see," Running Fox said, smiling at each of them. "That is good."

"I still believe that the white woman should not join us," one of his warriors blurted out. "Her presence will draw undue attention our way."

"Look at Nancy," Running Fox said, gesturing toward her with a hand. "Does she look anything at all like the woman who once rode with the whiskey peddler? With her long black hair, her tan, and her Indian attire such as our women wear, and especially without her eyeglasses, does she not look like a Lakota woman?"

"*Ay-uh*, that is so," the one who argued with Running Fox said. "That is part of the problem. No woman rides with a Lakota search party, ever."

"I will remedy that," Running Fox said, smiling over at Nancy. "She will dress like a warrior as she rides with us, not like a woman. Go to your lodges and prepare for departure," Running Fox ordered. "My *mitawin* and I will go to mine and prepare ourselves."

The warriors nodded and left for their own tepees while Nancy went with Running Fox to his.

Soon Nancy had on the clothes of a warrior, larger than what she would have liked, but secured tightly enough around her waist with a rope that they would not slide off her body.

Running Fox placed a band around her head such as he himself wore.

Then he gave Nancy some leaves of the wintergreen plant to chew. "This will calm you, for I see in your eyes that you are nervous," he said softly.

Nancy hesitated as she gazed down at the plant. Then she placed it in her mouth and chewed it. She found the taste close to that of wild spearmint.

"We will go to the trading post first to question them about whether or not they have heard news about your mother," he said, drawing her into his embrace before leaving. "All gossip leads there."

Nancy clung to him. "Now that it's time to actually leave for the search, I'm nervous," she said, her voice breaking. She gazed into his eyes. "Please— hold me for a moment longer?"

He brushed soft kisses across her lips, then held her tightly for a while. When they heard voices outside the tepee and the neighing of horses, they both knew that the warriors were waiting on their steeds, ready for action.

Running Fox held Nancy at arm's length. "You will be all right," he said, gazing intently into her eyes. "Remember the moment you downed the lynx and saved my life? That should give you the courage to do what must be done now for the sake of someone you love."

"I do love her," Nancy choked out. "When she was married to my father and we lived on the farm as a happy family, she was so different from the way she is now. Her change is all because of Joe's influence—all bad."

"Your *ina* will be happy again," Running Fox said softly.

"Then you do believe we will find her?" Nancy asked, wiping tears from her eyes. "You speak so positively."

"We will do what we can," Running Fox said, thrusting a rifle into her hand. "This is yours. Place it in the gun boot of your horse. You know how to use it if you are threatened."

"Do you think we might be?" Nancy said shakily, her hand trembling as she held the heavy rifle.

"We shall soon see," Running Fox said, placing his sheathed knife at his waist, then picking up another rifle.

It was not the best of times to travel with a bow and arrow. The rifle was the quickest way to protect oneself.

They stepped outside and saw all of the warriors readied for travel, their wives and children standing back, silently watching.

Nancy went to her steed, slid the rifle into the gun boot, and mounted the horse. Then she rode from the village with the warriors, Running Fox and herself in the lead.

She looked heavenward and silently prayed for a miracle!

Chapter 27

Nancy could not help but be somewhat jittery when she and Running Fox stepped into the trading post, a rustic cabin surrounded by cottonwood trees, with a small stream on its right side.

The other Lakota warriors waited outside on their horses.

Nancy saw the trading post agent look over the counter at her, past the many pelts and other items that had recently been brought in for trade.

Nancy tensed as the agent looked at her appraisingly and then stared intently into her eyes.

She had forgotten to worry about that—violet eyes were rare among white women, much less among Indians.

Running Fox saw the silent interest in the man's eyes and also realized why.

He had thought he was prepared for the visit, but only now did he realize that he had forgotten about Nancy's eyes, how unusual their color was.

He knew that he must get quickly to the issue at hand, or the discussion might go in a different direction from what he wanted.

"I am certain you are familiar with the name Whiskey Joe," Running Fox said, stepping over to obscure Nancy as best he could.

"Yes, and what about him?" the agent grunted, sweeping his stringy red hair out of his golden eyes. "What do you want to know about that scalawag?"

Nancy smiled at that reference to her stepfather. She knew there was no love lost between Whiskey Joe and the trading post agent.

"Have you received word of his wife's disappearance?" Running Fox asked as the man lit a long-stemmed pipe, which Running Fox knew had been traded from some Indian, possibly a Lakota warrior. It was made of the same sort of catlinite as his own. He focused on the man again.

"Do you know anything about the disappearance?" he asked once more.

"Yeah," the man finally said, lowering the pipe from his mouth. "I heard about the woman's disappearance, as well as her daughter who everyone knows as Naughty Nancy."

Running Fox stiffened at that name.

He fought hard against looking at Nancy to see her response.

"Some say that both abductions might be the work of the Chippewa," the agent said dryly.

Of course both Running Fox and Nancy knew that was not true.

And as for the Chippewa, Running Fox truly didn't believe that Chief Winter Moon would go back on his word and avenge the deaths of his two young braves. He had said that it was best to wait and see what Whiskey Joe's next move might be.

No. Running Fox knew that this man was only speculating about what might have happened. He knew nothing as fact.

Then a man that neither Running Fox or Nancy had seen because he had been standing back among the tall stacks of pelts came out into the open. He was smoking a cigar, the tip glowing orange in the semidarkness of that gloomy part of the room.

"I have the information you are seeking," the man said, moving into the light. He was a neatly dressed man, his hair cropped short to just above his snow-white shirt collar, his black suit neatly pressed.

"And what information is that?" Running Fox said as he turned toward the man. Nancy turned as well, staying close to Running Fox's side.

"I know about the older lady, but not the

younger one," the man said, flicking ashes from his cigar onto the thin layer of mud that had dried on the oak flooring.

Nancy's heart skipped a beat.

She so anxiously wanted to question him herself.

"What do you know?" Running Fox asked, resting a hand on his sheathed knife at his right side.

"She is being held captive against her will because she's refused to perform at the Crystal Palace," the man said evenly. "Her very own husband is holding her hostage, but no one knows where."

"And how would you know such information?" Running Fox asked, searching the man's eyes to see truth or lies in their depths. He saw truth.

"I visit the Crystal Palace from time to time, but not to see the performances," the man said. "I have dealings with Joseph Brock in the back room. We gamble. While gambling last night, he drank one shot of whiskey too many and absently told me about how he'd finally got rid of the two women in his life who were nothing but trouble to him. He said Naughty Nancy left on her own one night, but that he had full control of what happened to her mother. He told me that he was holding her hostage, but I couldn't get it outta him where, although I tried. He clamped up and said no more to me 'bout it."

It took all of Nancy's willpower not to speak up

and try to force answers out of him. She believed he did know more than he was telling.

She knew that it was best not to draw attention to herself, but she was so infuriated that her step-father could do this to her mother, she found it hard not to speak her mind.

"And you did not take this information to the authorities?" Running Fox asked.

"I steer clear of the law, if you get my drift," the neatly dressed man said. "I was accused of swin-dling someone at cards. After that, I learned to lay low."

"Yet you gave me information today," Running Fox said, his jaw tight.

"You ain't the law, now are you?" the man said, chuckling.

"No, I am not the law," Running Fox said.

"I wish I could help you some more," the man said. Then he forked an eyebrow. "Why are you so interested in the missing lady? She's nothing but a whore."

Running Fox gave the man a steady stare, then turned and left the trading post, Nancy at his side.

"Do you think you can trust anything he said?" Nancy asked. "Do you think Joe actually has my mother hidden somewhere?"

"We will do what we can to find answers," Run-ning Fox said. He turned to her. "I will do what I can to find your mother."

She flung herself into his arms. "Thank you," she said, a sob lodging in her throat.

He hugged her for a moment, then helped her onto her steed and mounted his own.

They rode away from the trading post, the other warriors on each side of them, unaware of the two white men out on the porch watching them as they left.

Who was the lovely thing with the Injun? Why was she dressed in male garb? Was she actually a white woman passing herself off as Indian, and if so, why? They wondered all these things.

They agreed that she had pretty eyes, then concluded that she must be one of those nasty breeds.

They shrugged and went back inside the trading post to continue with their business.

As for Nancy, she was stunned over what her stepfather reportedly had done to her mother.

She turned to Running Fox. "If it's true, and my stepfather is guilty of my mother's disappearance, I know almost for certain where she is," she blurted out. "There's a hidden cellar where he hides the largest portion of his most expensive alcohol. But it is kept under lock and key."

She smiled shrewdly. "There are only two people who know where the key is kept. I am one of the two, and the other is my stepfather. I've been with him many times when he has gone to restock his wagon before heading out to peddle his wares.

Running Fox, I'm almost certain that cellar is where we will find my mother."

"Where is this place?" Running Fox said, sidling his horse over closer to hers. "Is it guarded?"

"No, nobody guards it," Nancy said, recalling the many times she had gone inside the shack with her stepfather.

"It's a ramshackle shack a short distance from Dry Gulch," she said. "It's well hidden in a forest of spruce, birch, and oak trees. It's so well hidden and so far off the beaten path that no one would ever venture there. But someone who did happen along and see it would think it was just a place that one gust of wind might topple. Even if they ventured inside, they'd only see dirt and cobwebs. They would have no idea that in the cellar of that shack is expensive whiskey. No one would ever expect anything to be there that was worth the amount of money my stepfather's stash of whiskey is worth."

Running Fox looked heavenward and saw that the sun was almost at the horizon. Soon it would be dark.

He glanced at Nancy. "It is best that we do this at night," he said. "We will go and hide close to the shack, then when it is dark, we will make our move."

He wheeled his horse to a stop and faced his warriors. He quickly explained his plan to them, and then they all rode again in the direction of Dry Gulch.

When Nancy knew they were close to the shack, she put a hand out to halt Running Fox. "It's over there," she said, nodding toward a break in the trees a short distance away.

Running Fox nodded. Then he looked over his shoulder and gestured to his warriors.

Nancy stiffened as they made their way into the forest that was scented by the pine and spruce trees.

Running Fox drew a tight rein, stopped, and gazed over his shoulder at two of his warriors. "Stay," he said. "Keep watch. You know what to do if someone comes, especially Whiskey Joe."

They nodded.

Running Fox, Nancy, and the others rode ahead and dismounted in a thick stand of cottonwood trees. From there they could keep an eye on the shack.

When darkness shrouded the land, Running Fox and Nancy went ahead to the shack while the others kept watch.

Nancy prayed that she would be reunited with her mother in a matter of moments. If that could happen, she would do everything in her power to see that her mother was safe forever, too—and loved.

When they reached the shack, the moon's glow

streaming down from the dark heavens, Nancy led Running Fox inside.

She shivered as she made her way through the strings of cobwebs, but finally she found the kerosene lamp that she knew Joe kept there. She also knew where the matches were hidden. She lit the lamp and whispered, "Running Fox, follow me. The trap-door that leads down below is in the back room."

They entered the back room, where a rag rug stretched out from beneath a bed. The mattress was yellowed and smelled of skunk.

Joe kept the foul mattress there as a deterrent to anyone who might happen along and want to spend a night under a roof instead of under the open sky.

No one would be able to tolerate the strong stench. She could hardly stand it now as she helped Running Fox scoot the bed aside and throw the rug across the room.

"That's it," Nancy said, staring at the trapdoor, which was bolted shut.

"The key," she said, her fingers trembling as she reached under the bed and found it secured there on a nail.

Smiling victoriously, she handed it to Running Fox.

Soon Running Fox had managed to unlock the trapdoor, and he and Nancy peered into the darkness.

Nancy's heart skipped a beat when she heard something akin to mumbling from down below.

"Oh, Lord, it must be my mother," she said, a sob catching in her throat.

She handed the lamp quickly to Running Fox, then rushed down the rickety steps.

Again she heard the mumbling.

It was coming from somewhere to her right.

She stepped gingerly across the earthen floor, then gasped when she found her mother sitting on the cold floor, gagged, her wrists and ankles tied.

Nancy's knees grew rubbery with alarm when she saw how emaciated, dirty, and scared her mother was. She gasped when she saw several bites on her mother's face.

"Mama, oh, Mama," Nancy sobbed as she fell to her knees beside her mother.

She twined her arms around her neck and hugged her. "Mama, what has he done to you?"

Collecting her wits, Nancy untied the gag at her mother's mouth, while Running Fox used his knife to cut the ropes at her wrists and ankles.

Freed, Carole flung her arms around Nancy and clung to her. "Thank the Lord, child, oh, thank the Lord you came," she cried. "How did you know?" Then her eyes swept over Nancy. "And—what do you have on, Nancy? What have you done to your hair?"

She gave Running Fox a questioning stare. "And what are you doing with him?" she gasped.

"I'll tell you all about it later," Nancy said. "All you need to know now is that this is Running Fox and in a sense he saved my life—and is now saving yours."

"Running Fox?" Carole said, her eyes widening. "The young Lakota chief? How—? Why—?"

"Mama, please," Nancy said. "You've more important things to do now than to ask me so many questions."

"But—but—" Carole stammered.

"Mama!" Nancy said. "Please!"

Running Fox helped Carole to her feet, but her strength was not enough to hold her up.

"I'm so weak," she said with a sob. "And hungry. He hasn't brought me food since he placed me here. He's—he's a demon, Nancy. I should've listened to you."

"The bites on your face, Mama," Nancy said, studying them. "What sort are they?"

"Spiders," her mother gulped out, then raised the hem of her dress and revealed more bites there. "These were made by a rat that is hiding over there behind the whiskey."

Nancy exchanged glances with Running Fox. Then Nancy again questioned her mother. "Why did he bring you here?" she asked softly. "Was it because you wouldn't perform?"

"It was mainly because I wouldn't agree to make the whiskey runs with him," Carole said as she glanced at Running Fox. "Although he had promised both the Lakota and the Chippewa that he wouldn't peddle his whiskey among the Indians anymore, he was lying. As far as I know, he's even gone to an Indian village since he put me here. I do know that he loaded up one of his wagons just before he left me."

Nancy gasped and looked quickly at Running Fox, whose jaw had tightened at that information. "He never meant anything he said," she said, her voice breaking. "Running Fox, he lied. He—lied—"

Running Fox's eyes narrowed as he looked slowly around the room, at all of the whiskey. Then he smiled darkly at Nancy. "We will give him more than one surprise when he arrives here again," he said grimly. "Not only will your mother be gone, but his store of whiskey as well."

"What are you going to do?" Nancy asked, searching his eyes.

He gave her a determined look, seized a whiskey bottle, and emptied it on the cellar floor.

Realizing he needed to get the ladies out of the cellar, he escorted Nancy and Carole out of the shack and into the cool night air.

Several of his warriors then joined him in the cellar, where they emptied all of the whiskey until there was a river of it across the earthen floor.

They finished by breaking the jugs, then hurried outside.

Running Fox helped Nancy's mother mount his steed, then climbed up behind her.

Nancy's bitterness toward her stepfather had grown in intensity tonight.

But his whiskey was destroyed.

That would stop him for a good while now. But she knew that more radical measures would have to be taken when he got more of the spirit water from those who supplied him with it.

For now, it was just so good that she had found her mother and saved her.

And her mother now truly knew the evil of the man she had married.

They were both rid of him now!

As they rode back to the village, Nancy studied how tenderly Running Fox was holding her mother against his chest.

She loved this man so much, and she was so glad that her mother would know him too. Nancy would see to it that her mother stayed safe with her now that she had rescued her from Joe's prison.

Chapter 28

It was a cool, cloudy day as Nancy emerged from the tepee on Ghost Island.

She and her mother had come there after Medicine Bear had medicated Carole's bites at the main village.

Running Fox had brought them to the island but had left almost immediately so that he could be at the main village in case her stepfather had figured out who had taken Carole from the cellar and ruined his liquor supply.

"Nancy . . ."

Carole's weak voice calling her name snapped Nancy out of her reverie.

She hurried back inside the tepee and knelt beside her mother. Carole's face and hands were white with some sort of ointment that Medicine

Bear had placed there for the bites that her mother had suffered while in the cold, dank, and filthy cellar.

"What is it, Mama?" Nancy asked, smoothing her mother's hair back from her brow. Carole's hair was dyed red, as Nancy's had been.

"Joseph—" her mother gulped out, her eyes wild with fear. "If he discovers where we are, he'll—"

"He will be helpless to do anything about it," Nancy said soothingly. "Surely he knows better than to oppose Running Fox."

"But he can bring the authorities, or worse yet, the cavalry, saying Running Fox abducted both of us," Carole said, wincing when pain shot through the worst of the bites on her face.

"He wouldn't dare," Nancy assured her. "He was the one who abducted you and placed you in the cellar. One look at you would be proof enough of what happened. And I would speak in our behalf and tell the full story about that evil man. No, I doubt he would chance bringing the law onto Lakota land, for he surely would know that he would be the loser."

"I can't help but be afraid," Carole said, reaching for Nancy's hand.

"Mama, you are safe on Ghost Island. You know as well as I that no white people have ever set foot on this island because they fear it so much."

"Ghost Island?" Carole gasped, visibly shivering at the thought. "Is that where I am?"

"I didn't tell you before because I knew you would be afraid. But I want to reassure you how safe you are."

"Are there ghosts here?" Carole asked, her eyes wide as she peered into Nancy's. She was still surprised to see that Nancy no longer had to wear eyeglasses in order to see.

When Carole had realized that, she had thought the Lakota had performed some mystical magic or voodoo that made it possible for Nancy to see now without the aid of eyeglasses. She was relieved when she heard the real reason—that it had been a blow to her daughter's head that had brought her eyesight back to her, yet had not injured her in any way.

"Mama, there is no such thing as ghosts," Nancy said, smiling sweetly down at her. "You are safer here on this island than you would be anywhere. Trust me. I know. I was brought here the very night Running Fox stole me from my bed. I have never seen or heard any apparitions. Mama, I have never felt this safe anywhere. I was constantly afraid when I was living under the same roof as Joe. You don't know it, but I wished for a lock on my bedroom door every night because—because I thought he might come and defile me. I had seen him look at me so oddly at times, I took it as lust."

"I must admit that I too worried about that," Carole said, lowering her eyes. "I feel so ashamed that I did nothing about the possibility. I should have taken you away from that place the moment I knew what Joe's intentions for you were—that you would be used to help sell his whiskey and . . . to bring men into his Crystal Palace, and—worst of all—that he might climb into your bed some night and take from you what I often refused him."

"You refused him?" Nancy asked, startled by this confession. "Mama, you defied him in bed?"

"I tried to put on a good front for you, Nancy. I pretended that I loved him—because I was so afraid of him," Carole said, tears making paths now through the ointment on her face. "If you could have seen how he yanked his belt from his breeches on those most horrid of nights, and how he would stand there and slap the belt against his hand as he glared down at me, you would know that I was too afraid of a beating not to do anything he asked of me. I eventually stopped refusing him, especially when it occurred to me one night that he might leave my bed and go to yours and get from you what I didn't want to give him."

"My word!" Nancy gasped, paling. "And all along I thought you were so blinded by love that you would do anything for him."

"After you left I was even more afraid, but I could take only so much of what he did, and that was when he took me to the cellar. He hoped I would die without him actually having to kill me himself," Carole sobbed. "Had you not come—"

"But I did, Mama," Nancy said, sobbing herself as the horrible truths came to light. All along, Joe had forced many things on her mother that now, to Nancy, seemed unbearable to think about.

The fact that her mother had done everything she did to protect Nancy touched her deeply and made her love her mother more than she ever had.

"And you are dressed as an Indian," Carole said, her eyes moving slowly over Nancy. "Even your hair?"

"Yes. I washed the dye out as soon as I could after having arriving here," Nancy explained. "And I love the braid. Do you like it, Mama?"

"Nancy, you have never looked as pretty as now," Carole said, smiling. "And that handsome warrior. Ah, he's a saint, Nancy, a saint."

"Mama, we are in love," Nancy blurted out. "I am going to marry Running Fox."

Carole's eyes widened again. "You are going to marry an Indian?" she gasped. "Nancy, I—"

"Mama, he is more a man than any white man I have ever known, except for Papa, of course," Nancy said, stroking her mother's hair lovingly. "He is the kindest man, so sincere, and I do love him so much, as does he love me."

"But he is Indian," Carole insisted.

"So he is," Nancy said, sighing. "And he has given me a new life—a true purpose to live. Until he came into my life, I had given up on anything good ever happening for me. I felt utterly trapped."

"I know the feeling," Carole said, taking Nancy's hand. "And, Daughter, if you love that man, and he loves you, you have my blessing. He has done me a great service by rescuing me. I shall admire him for all eternity."

"And he and I will bring grandchildren into the world for you to hold and marvel over," Nancy said, smiling broadly. "And we will have many. I know how empty you must have felt when you were told that you could have no more children. Well, I shall make that up to you, Mama. You will have several to sing your lullabies to."

"I so loved singing to you when you were small," Carole said, tears again streaming from her eyes. "That was a lifetime ago."

"Yes, a lifetime," Nancy murmured. "Oh, Mama, I know how much you must miss Papa. I do, too. He was so wonderful to us. Oh, how I loved watching him plow the fields." She laughed softly. "Remember how angry he could get when the horses got stubborn and wouldn't pull the plow another inch?"

"Yes, they were as stubborn as mules some-times," Carole said, then turned toward the entrance flap as voices came closer to the tepee, one a man's, the other a woman's.

Nancy also heard.

She went to the entrance flap and held it aside, smiling when she saw Running Fox. Her smile faltered slightly when she saw Soft Star with him, for it was not her time to be on Ghost Island.

She stepped outside, lowered the flap, and went to Running Fox and Soft Star.

Running Fox swept her into his arms, then placed his hands on her shoulders and held her at arm's length.

"Your stepfather knows that it was I who asked about your mother's whereabouts, and word was brought to me that he is trying to find enough men to come to my village to retaliate," Running Fox said tightly. "He must have figured out that if it was I asking about your mother it was I who destroyed his whiskey supply before taking her away."

"No!" Nancy gasped, her heart skipping a beat. "Do you think he has put two and two together and realized that it was I who was with you that day? The one man at the trading post, the one in charge, probably realized who I was after I left."

"Nothing was said about you, so I doubt you were included in the conversation," Running Fox said. "And I am surprised that the man in charge of the trading post cooperated with your stepfather by telling him anything. Not only could he fear retaliation from me and my warriors, but also he knows the worth of our pelts. He would not like to lose our trade. I must go later and question him. If he does not give me the correct answers, he will no longer have trade from me or any of my warriors. I shall even go and spread this news to Chief Winter Moon. His pelts will be kept from that man as well."

"You came here to tell me this—and now what are you going to do?" Nancy asked, searching his eyes. "Whatever it is, I want a role in it. This all started because of my stepfather, and I want to be a part of his comeuppance."

"I believe he will arrive, to try and come and avenge what happened to his whiskey supply," Running Fox said gravely.

"Yes, I am certain it is only the whiskey that he is angry about," Nancy said. "He wouldn't care a hoot that you took my mother off his hands. He probably even said aloud the words 'good riddance' once he discovered that she was gone."

She gazed at Soft Star. "You have left the main village to come with Running Fox to Ghost Island," she said softly. "Why, Soft Star? Your place is at the main village until your husband returns for his duties here."

"I have come to sit with your mother and to pre-

pare her food while you are gone," Soft Star said
softly.

Nancy looked quickly at Running Fox. "While I
am gone?" she said, forking an eyebrow.

"I knew that you would want to be with me at
the main village when your stepfather arrived,"
Running Fox said, gently placing a hand on her
cheek. "I knew that you would want to be there
when he is taken captive."

"Yes, I truly do want to be there," Nancy said
softly. "But I am surprised that you—"

"*Mitawin,* I know you well," Running Fox said,
interrupting her. "So go now and say farewell to
your mother, but do not tell her why you are leaving. No need in worrying her. Just tell her that you
want to go to the main village to get supplies for
your stay here at Ghost Island."

"Yes, that should work," Nancy said, grateful
that he was being so generous to her about this
when he would much prefer that she stay out of the
upcoming fray.

But nothing would keep her from seeing her
stepfather forced to beg for mercy when he was en-
circled by Running Fox's warriors.

She could hardly wait to see the fear in his eyes,
for he had placed the same fear in her mother's
eyes.

"Go now. Explain the situation to your mother
and introduce her to Soft Star," Running Fox said,

twining his arms around Nancy's waist and drawing her into his embrace. "My *mitawin*, I promise you that soon the ordeal with your stepfather will finally be a thing of the past for both you and your mother. He has not much time left on this earth."

"You are going to kill him outright?" Nancy asked, her voice guarded.

"Not exactly," Running Fox said. He chuckled. "Go and speak to your mother. We must get back to the main village and be there should he arrive."

Nancy hugged him, then rushed back inside the tepee. Soft Star stayed outside to give Nancy time to explain to her mother what was happening.

"I shan't be gone long," Nancy told her mother. "And when I return, you're going to see how much I've learned about cooking."

"You can cook?" Carole asked, her eyes widening. "Daughter, that was something you ran from when we lived on the farm. You preferred to be outside with your father rather than in the kitchen making pies and biscuits."

"I still don't know how to make them, but I can make a zesty venison stew," Nancy said with a laugh. "Mama, I'm going to introduce you to someone who is going to be with you until I return. She's lovely. You are going to love having her with you."

"What is her name?" Carole asked.

"Soft Star."

"What a lovely name."

"A lovely name for a lovely woman," Nancy said. She bent over and gave her mother a kiss.

She opened the entrance flap and motioned for Soft Star to come in.

Soon Nancy and Running Fox set off in his canoe in the direction of the main village for their final confrontation with Joe.

Soon he would pay for every dirty deed he had ever done.

Chapter 29

Nancy fidgeted as she waited in Running Fox's tepee for the possible arrival of her stepfather.

As far as she knew, no one had spied him coming, and there were many sentries posted in the most strategic of places to keep an eye out for him.

She looked up as Running Fox came into the tepee.

"We might be wrong about Joe," she said. "I would have thought he would have arrived by now. Maybe he couldn't get enough people to accompany him here. Surely they know the repercussions would be bad."

"There are many white men who would take any opportunity to fight the redskins, especially if they think they can truly leave a slaughter behind," Running Fox said.

He knelt beside Nancy and lifted a log onto the fire, then settled down on a pallet of furs beside the fire.

He reached for her hand. "You know that slaughters have happened often in the history of the red man, and the white lawmen have always turned their eyes another way, so as not to say they knew about such killings," he said. "Most white lawmen, especially the white pony soldiers, are snakes, not humans."

"That's horrible," Nancy said, shuddering.

"But the lawman at Dry Gulch is not that sort of man," Running Fox reassured her. "If he receives word about what Whiskey Joe might be trying to do, he will stop him. But I am almost certain that Joe knows this and will try hard to conceal his plans from the sheriff and his deputies."

"I hope you're right about the sheriff," Nancy said. "I can't help but be somewhat apprehensive about all of this. I am so worried that it even feels as though something is crawling along my flesh."

"That will pass soon." Running Fox put a comforting arm around her waist and drew her close to him. "Soon this will be behind us and we can concentrate on more pleasant things."

"Our marriage," Nancy said, sighing blissfully at the thought of being his wife. "And then children."

She leaned away from him and gazed into his eyes. "I told Mama that she can expect many grandchildren to sing her lullabies to," she said, excitement in her voice.

"Did the news please her?" Running Fox asked, searching her eyes.

"Very much," Nancy murmured. She took Running Fox's hands in hers. "We had such a nice talk about everything. I know things now that I didn't know before. My stepfather forced her to do things that she didn't want to do. Until today, I didn't know the sordid details."

"She—"

Running Fox started to say something but stopped when he heard shouts outside his lodge. His scouts were reporting that Whiskey Joe and many white men on horses had been seen riding hard toward the village.

"As planned, they are coming," Running Fox said, leaping to his feet.

He went to his store of weapons and brought out two rifles.

He gave one to Nancy, keeping the other for himself.

"Stay inside the tepee until Whiskey Joe and his men are surrounded and they can do nothing to harm you," he said firmly.

Nancy gulped and nodded.

Running Fox placed a hand on her cheek. "Soon this will all be over."

"I hope so," Nancy said softly, trying to push

away the thought of perhaps inheriting the trait of her mother, who could only have one child. What if Nancy could have none at all?

She had not allowed herself to think about that, not until now, and when she might soon be with child.

She had missed her monthly by two weeks now.

That could mean she was pregnant already.

Or was it too soon to know?

She would pray every morning and every evening that she was with child and that she could give her beloved Running Fox a son.

Running Fox brushed a soft kiss across her lips, then stepped outside and waited.

The wait was not long.

Soon he spied the white men, Whiskey Joe in the lead, walking into the village with their wrists tied behind their backs, surrounded by many of Running Fox's trusted warriors.

Running Fox stood stiffly facing them, his eyes filled with anger.

As Joe was shoved closer to Running Fox, Running Fox glared into his eyes, then into the eyes of the others who were with him, some of whom he recognized from having seen them on the streets of Dry Gulch.

Some of the men with Joe he would have never thought brave enough to fight Running Fox and his warriors.

Then there were some whom he would have trusted, but who now stood with their eyes lowered shamefully, their chins trembling.

But Joseph Brock stood with defiance in his eyes as he glared back at Running Fox.

"You are a tricky sonofabitch," Joe growled. "How'd you know I was gunning for you?"

"You are a fool to think I would not hear of it," Running Fox said icily. "You were a fool to lie to both me and Chief Winter Moon about never bringing spirit water among us again."

"But I didn't," Joe said, his voice turning into a whine.

"Are you saying that you were not even planning to?" Running Fox said stiffly. "Are you daft enough to stand there with my warriors all around you and lie to my face about what you were planning?"

"I did not lie," Joe said, his voice breaking. "I would have never brought whiskey among you or Chief Winter Moon's people again."

Nancy listened and heard it all.

She had had enough.

Suddenly she stepped outside and took her place beside Running Fox, gripping a rifle in her right hand.

She saw the color drain from her stepfather's face as he gaped openly at her.

"Hello, Joe," Nancy said, placing a fist on her

hip. "Are you happy to see your stepdaughter again? Are you anxious to see your wife?"

"Nancy?" he choked out, his eyes taking in her Indian attire and the normal color of her hair.

He gasped when he saw that she didn't need eyeglasses to see, for she was looking directly at him without them.

"Nancy," he repeated. "What are you doing here? And—and—where are your eyeglasses? And what did you say about your mother? Where is she?"

She laughed out loud, noting the fiery anger that slowly filled his eyes as he realized he had been duped.

"You are a stupid man," she said. "Do you want to know how Running Fox knows that you are lying through your teeth about trading whiskey to the Indians again? My mother. When we found Mother in the cellar with the whiskey, she told me why she was there. She said she refused to accompany you on your whiskey runs to the Indians and that was why you threw her in that pit of hell with rats and spiders, all of which took bites of her."

"That witch," Joe snarled. "I knew I should've shut her up once and for all. Because of her, my whiskey supply was destroyed, and now I'm dog food for these savages."

"Well, you are almost right about that," Running Fox said, laughing at what Joseph had just said.

"But I will not go as far as serving you on a platter to dogs—if you will notice, you'll see that our village has no dogs. But we do have a place where we will take you that is much better than how you described your end would be."

Nancy was enjoying watching her stepfather squirm, and she smiled when she saw just how pale he had become.

"What are you planning to do with me and the other men?" Joe gulped out, trembling. "Please have mercy. I apologize for lying to you." He looked quickly at Nancy. "I apologize for what I did to you, and, oh, Lord, your mother. You said she got bit. Did she die? Did she live only long enough to tell you my plans?"

"I'm sure you wish that she had died, but no, she's very much alive and she will be happy to see you begging for mercy," Nancy said dryly.

"Where is she?" Joe prodded, looking past Nancy at Running Fox's tepee. "Is she in there? Can I see her? I want to tell her I love her and that I'm sorry."

"She isn't there," Nancy said stiffly. "And if she was, I wouldn't let you lie to her again. You have never loved her. You only married her for what you could get from both of us."

"You said she was alive, so, damn it, where is she?" Joe said angrily.

"She's on Ghost Island," Nancy said, eager to see

his response to that, since she knew the dread even the words "Ghost Island" brought to all white people's eyes.

"Ghost . . . Island . . . ?" Joe gasped. "She is at Ghost Island?"

"Yes, and that is where I am taking you and the other men who foolishly aligned themselves with you," Running Fox said.

He angrily grabbed Joe by an arm and shoved him in the direction of the lake.

"Walk, white man," he growled. "Walk to the canoes that are beached and ready for you."

"No, oh, Lord, no," Joe cried, while the rest of the men, too afraid to speak, stared blankly at Running Fox.

A warrior stepped up to Joe and began dragging him toward the lake. Other warriors followed his lead and forced the other white men toward the shore.

Nancy joined Running Fox in his canoe. Soon the moans of fear were filtering through the thick fog as the canoes made their way to the island.

When they reached shore, night was already spreading its dark shroud over the island, making it even more eerie and ghostly in appearance. Soon the warriors had taken the white men to the burial ground, where they lay prone, their ankles and wrists secured to the ground by stakes.

The moon shone down on them, revealing their fear as they gazed at Running Fox.

"You savage! You damn savage!" Joe howled, as he strained against the ropes at his wrists and ankles. "You'll burn in hell for doing this."

Running Fox laughed loosely. "After one night here amid the graves of my ancestors, you will be speaking a different language," he said.

Nancy saw Joseph's eyes widen in disbelief as Carole was brought to where she could see him.

She was supported on both sides by warriors since her knees were still too weak to hold her up.

"Finally, Joe, you are up against people who will stand their ground against you," Carole said in as strong a voice as she could manage.

"You are a double-crossing witch," Joseph growled. He gave Nancy, who was now at her mother's side, a sour look. "You too, Naughty Nancy."

"Yes, you would still call me that, even though you know it no longer means anything to me," Nancy said, smiling slowly. "Go ahead. Call me that again. See if I care."

"Naughty Nancy, Naughty Nancy, Naughty Nancy," Joseph ranted, over and over, trying to get the best of Nancy while he still could, angry when he saw that his taunting did not work.

In fact, she turned around and walked away with her mother and the warriors who were assisting her.

"Naughty Carole, Naughty Carole!" Joseph then shouted. "Just look at you, Naughty Carole! You're ugly as a skunk now!"

"Mama, ignore him," Nancy encouraged. "Don't let him know that he's getting the best of you. Mama, please don't give him the satisfaction of seeing you cry. Please!"

Her mother cleared her throat, then pulled free of the warriors. She wanted to walk without assistance, to show Joe that he had not conquered her in any respect.

Nancy laughed and walked with her mother back to the tepee, not bristling at all when Whiskey Joe continued to curse and rant at them.

Running Fox came into the tepee and helped Nancy's mother onto the pallet of pelts beside the fire, then drew Nancy into the comfort of his arms. "Soon you will never have to hear his voice again," he said, stroking Nancy's back through the doeskin dress. "*Mitawin*, soon it will all be over."

But even as he said that, she could still hear her stepfather calling both her and her mother by the nasty names, though the other men seemed more aware of what they had to fear, for they screamed and begged.

Nancy clung to Running Fox, shuddering at the ugliness of her stepfather's words.

Then the men went suddenly quiet. There came a sound that was louder than the men's screams and cries for mercy. From someplace hidden in the thickest part of the forest on Ghost Island, a wolf howled mournfully, answered by another and then another, until they all were united in a chorus.

"When the wolves howl like that, it is a sign of a coming storm," Running Fox said, gazing at the closed entrance flap, then at Nancy. "There were signs in the sky today, and now there are warnings from the wolves. There is no doubt that before another morning comes, there will be a storm."

"And what about the wolves?" Nancy asked, fear showing in the guardedness of her voice. "They seem so close. Do they sense the men's presence out there on the ground? Could they come and harm us?"

"Wolves are very wise. Their wisdom was given to them by the Great Spirit," Running Fox said. "I know of these wolves on our island. I have often heard their cries and have even seen their glittering eyes in the dark, but they keep their distance from the Lakota, as we keep ours from them."

"The cries are so hideous tonight," Nancy said, shivering.

"It is their way of communicating amongst themselves," Running Fox said. "To them it is beautiful, for they are relaying their feelings for one another with every howl."

"I imagine Joe fears them right now more than anything else," Nancy murmured.

"Soon he will have no sense of logic about anything," Running Fox said. "As I have already told you, soon all of this will be over."

Nancy gave him a questioning look, wondering where exactly this was all going to go—and what he had meant about Joe soon having no sense of logic about anything.

Running Fox said nonchalantly, "Soon we will have rain, thunder, and lightning, for there were too many signs today, both in the heavens, and now in the howls of the wolves, for it not to be so."

It was then that they saw the first flash of lightning overhead through the smoke hole, quickly followed by a loud clap of thunder.

Chapter 30

Nancy lay next to Running Fox, trembling as she listened to the incessant pounding of the rain against the buckskin covering of the tepee and the constant booms of thunder as lurid streaks of lightning continued to spark the dark heavens.

She clung to Running Fox, unable even to close her eyes, for more than the rain and thunder was keeping her awake.

It was the constant screams and moans from the men who were staked outside on the burial ground.

It was as though all spirits and ghosts had come from the graves to haunt them!

Nancy could not help but be afraid. "Running Fox," she whispered, gently shaking him by an arm. "Please wake up. I'm so afraid."

Running Fox sluggishly opened his eyes—nothing had disturbed him.

He felt Nancy's trembling and in the glow of what remained of their lodge fire he could see fear in her eyes.

He glanced over at her mother, who, thankfully, was asleep, oblivious of what was happening outside in the rain. She had been given a potion before she retired for the night, in order to help her to sleep through the pain of her bites, as well as the tormented cries from the men that Running Fox had imprisoned.

To prepare Nancy for the worst, he had explained everything to her—telling her how the men would persist throughout the night in begging to be released. But nothing seemed to have helped her.

"*Mitawin*, soon it will be morning, and all of this will be behind you," Running Fox said, drawing her even closer to him. "When a storm breaks at sunset, the weather is still unsettled in the morning, but if the sky clears during the night, or in the early-morning hours, we will then have settled weather. I shall hold you until the storm ceases and morning comes with its freshness."

She gazed at the closed entrance flap and noticed that it wasn't quivering and shaking in the wind any longer. The rain had suddenly stopped.

But the thunder and lightning continued far out

across the land, seemingly too stubborn to let up just yet, wanting to wait until morning before leaving this part of the country in peace.

"Those men," Nancy said, cuddling even more closely to Running Fox. "I have never heard such sounds as what they made through the night. But finally it's over. I hear them no more."

"Then try and get some rest before morning arrives," Running Fox encouraged. "Just close your eyes. Think of something pleasant that will make you smile. Think of the children we will have one day."

"Yes—children," Nancy said, smiling for the first time tonight. "Yes, I shall think of children."

But no matter how hard she tried, she couldn't get the men out of her mind's eye. She dwelled on how they must look out there, staked to the ground, soaked and chilled to the bone.

And she had to wonder what they might truly have seen.

Being out in the rain and cold surely would not have conjured up such sounds as she had heard coming from those men.

She did dread seeing them, for she knew she would see something horrible when she looked upon their faces.

Again she trembled.

"Forget everything, my *mitawin*, everything but being here in my arms and being thankful that you have your mother with you again and that she will survive the torturous bites that she got while imprisoned in the cellar," Running Fox whispered into her ear. "She is asleep now, safe, and far from any more danger that your stepfather could have inflicted on her. When you begin to pity him because of what might have become of him tonight, remember what he did to both you and your mother—and to the young braves of the Lakota and the Chippewa people. More than one of our youths are dead now because of his evil. He deserves no less than what has happened to him tonight."

"Yes, I know," Nancy murmured.

He brushed kisses across her brow. "*Ah-boo*, sleep, my pretty one. *Ah-boo*, sleep."

"Yes, sleep . . ." Nancy whispered, finally finding solace in sleep as it came to her so sweetly while being held in her lover's arms.

And then it seemed such a short sleep as the sun came through the smoke hole overhead and fell upon her face, awakening her.

She gazed up through the hole and saw light and fleecy clouds floating across the sky.

She found that Running Fox was already up and gone.

She looked over at her mother and saw that she was just stirring.

Nancy rose to her knees, crawled over to her mother, and took one of her hands in hers.

"Mama, how are you this morning?" she asked softly.

"I'm all right, but I had some terrible nightmares," Carole said, swallowing hard. "In them I heard the worst moans and groans, surely coming from someone dying, but I never saw who."

Icy fear squeezed at Nancy's heart as she looked at the entrance flap. Suddenly she was aware that she no longer heard sounds coming from the men.

"Mama, I'm going to go and see something," she said, scrambling to her feet.

She hurried to the entrance flap, stepped outside into the sweet morning air, then gazed at the burial grounds. She saw that the men were still there, prone on the ground, yet not making a sound or moving.

Running Fox saw her and hurried to her. "You might not want to see," he said, trying to encourage her to go back inside the tepee.

"Yes, I do," she said, stepping past him.

In her sleeping gown, she ran to the burial ground, then stopped and gasped and felt light-headed at what she saw.

The men were alive, but their eyes were wide and blank.

They were all soaked to the skin from the rain, and none of them seemed aware of anything.

They were now only ghosts of themselves.

Running Fox came and stood beside her.

He took her hand.

She turned and questioned him with her eyes. "What happened to them?" she asked, her voice breaking. "It seems that they are mindless."

"They will not harm anyone ever again," he said thickly. "Their sense of logic, of knowing, is gone. It has all been frightened away."

"They were frightened mindless?" Nancy gasped, gazing at her stepfather and finding it strange that he was not yelling at her or calling her by her nickname.

He was there, yet he wasn't.

"One will never know exactly what transpired here while we were safe inside our lodge," Running Fox said stiffly. "But the fact remains that those men are now harmless. Harmless."

Nancy swallowed hard, stunned to see her stepfather like this and realizing that he was truly mindless.

A part of her could not help but pity him.

And she would not allow herself to wonder about exactly what he and the others had witnessed while out there in the rain, lightning, and thunder.

It was something she did not want to know.

She turned to Running Fox again. "What is to become of them now?" she asked, her voice trembling.

"They will be released," Running Fox said nonchalantly.

"Released?" Nancy gasped. "Where? And having lost their minds, where will they go?"

"They will be taken from the island, far, far away from Dry Gulch and the families of those who know them," Running Fox said. He took her gently by an elbow and walked her back toward their tepee. "They will be set loose, to wander mindlessly on foot, wherever their wanderings take them."

"But as they are, no one will know how they came to be like this," Nancy said, taking one last look at her stepfather before going inside the tepee. "They can't tell anyone."

"That is the point," Running Fox said, smiling slowly at Nancy. "Your stepfather can no longer endanger the lives of our young ones by offering them spirit water."

"But the other men," Nancy said, inhaling a quavering breath. "They didn't deserve this as much as my stepfather did."

"They chose their fate the moment they sided with the whiskey peddler in defiance of the Lakota," Running Fox said matter-of-factly. "Their intentions were not pure toward us, or toward you and your mother. They are no less guilty of wrongs than your stepfather. They had to pay for siding with a man whose heart was led by evil."

"What are you talking about?" Carole asked, leaning up on an elbow. "How did Joe fare the night?"

"He's all right," was all that Nancy would tell her mother. "He's going to be taken from the island, but he will never threaten you again, Mama, nor I. That's all you need to know."

"Thank the Lord for that," Carole said, sighing as she once again lay down on the plush pelts, her eyes closing as she fell into another light sleep.

"I don't want her ever to know what truly happened to him," Nancy said softly. "There might be a part of her that would feel sad for the man, as I cannot help but pity him. It is best for her not to have any reason to think about it any longer."

"She will have no cause ever again to think about that man," Running Fox said, drawing Nancy into his embrace. "Nor will you."

He brought his lips down on hers in a soft kiss.

Chapter 31

Nancy felt as though she were floating on a cloud. The day had been so beautiful, and soon she would be Running Fox's bride! They had not seen each other all day while everyone else celebrated.

The feasting and dancing had begun almost at dawn.

Once Running Fox and Nancy became husband and wife, the day of celebration would be complete.

The Lakota people would disperse to their private lodges, as would all who had come by canoe from other villages.

Nancy and Running Fox would then celebrate their nuptials in their own special lodge that Running Fox had prepared for them a short distance from the village, beside the lake.

A young brave had been assigned to run ahead just when the music and drumming began, to light the fire inside the tepee so that it would be warm in the lodge when the newlyweds arrived to spend their night there.

Nancy was in Soft Star's tepee. Her mother sat close by beside a lodge fire, as Soft Star braided tiny white flowers, brought in from the forest, into Nancy's hair.

Nancy kept running her hands down the front of her wedding dress. It was so soft to the touch. She had thanked Soft Star repeatedly for the dress. Soft Star had secretly made the beautiful beaded doe-skin dress just for today's special moments between the woman who had become her best friend and her beloved chief.

As Nancy had hoped, her wedding dress had been made from the snow-white pelt that Chief Winter Moon had brought to Running Fox on the day they had come together as allies. This made her dress doubly special!

Running Fox was alone in his tepee at this very moment making final preparations before the nuptials.

"It's been a long day as I've waited for the moment to step outside for the wedding ceremony. Yet it doesn't seem that long because you two have kept me occupied with talking and your fussing over me," Nancy mused, smiling down at her mother, who also wore a doeskin dress and looked even younger than she usually did. Nancy was so glad that they had waited for her mother to heal before getting married. Her face was almost clear of the bites now.

"Daughter, you could never look more beautiful than you do today," Carole said, wiping tears from her eyes. "I was so tied up in myself and the drudgery of being that—that—man's wife, I had brushed you aside. Nancy, I promise never to do that again. I am here for you, always."

The flowers now in place in Nancy's hair gave off a lovely scent as Nancy bent low and brushed soft kisses across her mother's brow, then stood again over her, beaming.

"Mama, please forget everything ugly that came into our lives after Papa died. We are being given a second chance at happiness. Remember, Joseph Brock will never interfere in our lives again, especially our happiness."

"You are getting such a wonderful man," Carole said, pushing herself up from the floor.

She stood beside Nancy as Soft Star now braided flowers that matched Nancy's into Carole's long braid, the color now back to its normal golden since she had washed the dreadful red dye from it.

"I know," Nancy said, clasping her hands before her. "And he will be such a wonderful father."

Carole looked quickly at Nancy and saw how Nancy was resting her hand on her stomach.

She gazed into Nancy's eyes. "Are you saying what I think you are saying?" she asked, her lips quivering.

"I know now that I am with child," Nancy said, blushing. She knew that some would say she had sinned by having sexual relations before she had spoken vows with the father of the baby.

But the circumstances under which she had fallen in love with Running Fox were different from most meetings between a man and a woman who fell in love.

When he had taken her to his bed of blankets, it was as though he was giving her back her life.

When they had made love, all the ugliness of her past was erased.

As she had told Running Fox, it did seem as though she had been reborn.

"I shall babysit as often as you like, Nancy," Carole said, her eyes bright with happiness. She stifled a sob behind a hand. "It has been so long since I have held a baby in my arms. You—you—have no idea how I have ached for that. You grew up so quickly."

"Too quickly," Nancy said bitterly. "Because of the man you married, Mama. Because of Joseph Brock, I was forced to be older than my years as he pushed me out onto that terrible stage before those drunken bums."

"I am so sorry," Carole said, tears filling her eyes. "I doubt I can ever forgive myself."

"Oh, Mama, I shouldn't have brought it up— not today, when everything should be wonderful," Nancy cried, flinging herself into her mother's arms. "I'm sorry, Mama. Today is a miracle. Nothing should be said to darken it."

"One day we both will be able to forget those ugly years of our lives," Carole said, hugging Nancy to her. "Daughter, let us think of our happiness. This is the beginning of the rest of our lives."

"Yes, the rest of our lives," Nancy murmured.

She gave her mother one last hug, then looked toward the closed entrance flap when she heard a sudden silence outside the lodge and then the faint, yet constant, strumming of the drums, accompanied by the soft music from a handmade, carved *chatanka*, flute.

She turned excited eyes to Soft Star and then to her mother. "It is almost time!" she said, her voice filled with excitement. "He should be coming soon on his steed! Shortly after that we will be husband and wife!"

"It is good that the Chippewa accepted your invitations and came to join the celebration of love," Soft Star said, fussing one last time over Nancy's hair and dress. She placed a bouquet of flowers like those that had been twined into Nancy's hair into her hands. "Chief Winter Moon and many of his people sit among our people. That in itself is a miracle."

"I am so happy for Running Fox and Winter Moon, that they have come together in a bond unlike any other Lakota and Chippewa chiefs before them," Nancy said quietly. "We will go to the Chippewa village, too, when we are invited to special ceremonies and celebrations."

"Yes," Soft Star said. "We women love to get together to exchange knowledge of beading and cooking. I, especially, look forward to knowing some of their recipes. I do love to cook so much."

Nancy looked over at Soft Star and gave her a smile. "When I was a young girl who should have been interested in learning how to cook I was more involved in outdoor things with my papa. I loved helping him in the garden."

"But you hated hunting, so you never joined him in doing that," Carole said. "You wouldn't even touch a firearm, much less learn how to use one. Nor did you ever want to learn how to ride a horse. But now? You know how to do both. Cooking is the next thing for you to learn and enjoy. I look forward to being a student with you if Soft Star is willing to teach us together."

"I shall adore it," Soft Star said, clasping her hands eagerly.

"I am so excited that my knees are trembling," Nancy suddenly said. Then she giggled. "I will never forget this day. Never!"

In his tepee Running Fox smiled as he dressed and slipped on his porcupine-quill-embroidered moccasins.

He brushed his long, glossy hair one last time, then perfumed it with scented grass and carefully arranged it into two braids, with otter skin woven through them.

Wearing heavily beaded doeskin, he folded his best robe, made of bear fur, about him, then stepped outside, where a steed awaited him.

Today he would ride a sorrel horse streaked with black lightning.

He jumped onto its bare back, arranging a part of his robe under him to serve as a saddle. Then, holding the end of a lariat tied about the horse's neck, he guided the animal by the motion of his body. The steed's graceful movements were perfectly obedient to its master's needs.

As he rode toward the crowd around the huge outdoor fire, he spotted Chief Winter Moon and a good portion of his people, sitting among the Lakota.

Ay-uh, today was a fresh beginning for so many people with red skin. It was a wonderful beginning for the rest of his life with the woman he adored.

As he slowly approached Soft Star's lodge, he

pulled his robe over his head, leaving only a slit to look through.

He approached Nancy as she stepped from the lodge, looking beautiful, her violet eyes beaming.

His heart soared at the sight of her. Then he began to sing his courting song, which made tears of happiness fill her eyes.

He gazed at her through the tiny slit in the robe that covered him and sang, "*Hay-ay-ay! Hay-ay-ay! a-ahay-ay!* Listen! You will hear of him—Hear of him who loves you! Maiden, you will hear of him—Hear of him who loves you, who loves you! Listen! Listen, Mitawica, I take this woman for my wife. Listen, my *mitawin*, my wife, listen. Your husband will shortly sweep you away!"

Nancy listened appreciatively to the song and understood that he was singing it solely for her. Suddenly she realized that he had just said that he had taken her for his wife. Did their union come that simply? He sang to her and she was now his bride?

Yes! It did seem so, for he came at a faster lope now, his robe discarded and dropped on the ground. When he came up to her, he reached out for her and drew her onto the horse with him.

"We are now married?" she asked, her eyes wide. "There is no actual ceremony?"

"I am chief, so I can make our wedding day what I want it to be," Running Fox said happily. "I did not want to delay any longer knowing that you are my wife."

"I am your wife." She marveled at the reality of it. "You are my husband!"

"Yes, we are husband and wife," Running Fox said, acknowledging the loud cheers and chants as he wheeled his horse around and rode hard away from the crowd, into the forest, toward the tepee prepared for their first night as husband and wife.

Nancy could see a glow through the buckskin fabric and knew that a fire awaited them.

She could even smell food cooking over the lodge fire.

And when Running Fox dismounted, reached up for her and carried her inside, she was enchanted with what she saw. Flowers like those she had carried and wore in her hair were scattered across the floor, along the woven mats.

Incense of some sort floated overhead, like soft smoke, and from a huge pot hanging over the fire came the tantalizing aroma of venison.

Then she spied the bed that filled the whole back of the lodge, with the richest of pelts piled high, so soft-looking, so inviting.

"Do you approve?" Running Fox asked, still holding her in his arms.

"How could I not?" Nancy murmured.

She clung to his neck as he went to their bed, then bent low and laid her there.

She watched him slowly remove his clothes, even unwind his braids and toss aside the otter skins that had been woven into them.

She sucked in a quivering breath and felt a quickening yearning when he knelt beside her, lovingly removing her clothes until she was nude as well.

Soon their bodies came together like a beautiful song.

Running Fox reverently breathed her name against her lips, then ran little kisses across the nape of her neck, driving her almost wild with desire.

Then his mouth seized hers in a frenzied kiss as he enfolded her with his solid strength and sank his manhood deeply into her softly yielding folds.

She flung her arms around his neck and strained her body upward to meet his, the endlessly spiraling sweep of bliss rushing through her veins.

Happiness bubbled from deep within as he continued to kiss her, their bodies in tune with each other, Running Fox's groans of pleasure firing Nancy's passions even more.

He paused for a moment and studied her with eyes drugged with desire.

"I love you, wife," he said huskily. "I shall always love and protect you."

"My husband . . . ," Nancy said. Then she giggled.

"I can't believe I can say that and it is true! My husband!"

"It is true until there is no more breath in our bodies," Running Fox said. Then he kissed her almost wildly and desperately as he thrust himself rhythmically within her.

His body trembled with readiness.

He drove into her swiftly and surely, hugging her fiercely to him.

With a moan of ecstasy Nancy gave him back everything he was giving to her.

He held her close as she shuddered, arched, and cried out, and he too found his own ultimate pleasure.

Afterward, as Nancy lay at Running Fox's side, she sobbed.

He was startled.

He leaned up on an elbow and gazed in wonder at her tears. "Did I hurt you?" he asked anxiously.

"No, my darling," Nancy said through her tears. "These tears I am shedding tonight are tears of pure joy."

She reached for one of his hands. "Touch my belly," she said and placed his hand there. "I had told you that I might be with child?"

"*Ay-uh*, you did say that," Running Fox said, his heart skipping a beat with anticipation.

"Press an ear where your hand is and one day

you might be able to hear our baby's movements," Nancy said, her voice breaking with emotion.

Running Fox could hardly contain his excitement and pride, for he now knew for certain that she was with child—their child, born of their special, endearing love!

He eagerly pressed his ear against her warm belly, then smiled. "I look forward to hearing movement and knowing our child is there and eager to be born," he said. "It is such a good day for us. Not only are we now married, but we can speak of a child that will be born of our love."

"A son first, I hope," Nancy said tenderly.

"A daughter," Running Fox said, chuckling. "How could a daughter not be beautiful if she comes from inside you, the most beautiful woman in the world?"

Nancy blushed and giggled, then moved gently into his arms and melted as once again he kissed her and held her.

"Another magical day, another day of miracles," she said to herself.

Just how could one woman be this lucky?

Chapter 32

The full moon shone bright over Lake Michigan, where the Lakota warriors were hunting deer in canoes by torchlight.

Nancy had asked to go with Running Fox, but this time he had said that she shouldn't, for no women had ever accompanied the men in the canoes for these nighttime hunts. The women stayed in their lodges with the children, making certain none of them would get in the way of arrows that flew in the night from the powerful, sinew-backed bows.

Nancy was learning that now that she was a chief's wife, she had to be careful of asking for things that might make him feel awkward or look weak in the eyes of his warriors.

Tonight she had quickly agreed that her place was not in the canoe with her husband.

But she just hadn't been able to stay home like the other women.

She was too intrigued by how the warriors were hunting deer to stay away in the tepee and wait for Running Fox to return home with his kill.

She had gone to a high cliff and positioned herself so that she would be out of the danger of arrows but still able to see this interesting custom of the Lakota.

She now sat beneath the magnificent canopy of the night sky, spangled with stars, comfortable on a blanket that she had brought for herself. When she gazed heavenward, she had a sudden overwhelming sense of infinity, of God's universe, and of her own littleness by comparison.

But her world was wonderful now. She was content. She had never been happier.

Except for the splash of the water as the canoes swept through it and the twang of the bowstrings as arrows were shot from them, all was quiet.

Ah, how wonderful it was, she thought to herself, how sweet the night air was with the smell of the last wild roses of summer. A screech owl let out a quiet hoot as it rustled the leaves of a nearby cottonwood tree while seeming to be settling in for a long night's vigil.

Nancy looked over her shoulder and up into the

tree and saw the green shine of the owl's eyes, smiling when it let out another hoot, as though welcoming her to its domain.

She had read somewhere that Indians had a superstitious fear of that bird, believing that the spirit of the dead often appeared in that form.

But Nancy saw the owls in a different light. She saw them as beautiful, especially the barn owls that used to make their homes in her father's barn on the farm.

Again she watched the warriors, the torchlight bright enough for her to see when they shot arrows from their bows. She smiled when she heard one or more of them let out a loud whoop, which meant that the arrow had met its target.

All firing of arrows stopped as one canoe after another went ashore to find the downed deer and place it in a designated place, where all deer that were killed tonight were being laid until the night's hunt was over.

Then the deer would be loaded in the canoes and taken home, where the women waited, ready to dress them for future use.

Nancy knew that she didn't have much longer on the cliff, for she would be expected to be home, ready to do her part after the hunt.

She actually dreaded Running Fox's bringing home a deer. She had always loved animals, and it had been hard to help take the pelt from that first deer that he had brought home the day after their wedding ceremony.

She would never forget his wide smile as he had approached her.

When she had seen the blood, not only on the animal's lovely hide but also on Running Fox's clothes, and the death stare of the deer's big brown eyes, Nancy had suddenly gotten ill, but she had fought back the urge to vomit because she knew it would have embarrassed her husband for the others to see her weakness.

She had wanted to blame it on being pregnant, yet deep inside she knew that it was because she had hated seeing the lovely animal that had run free only a short while ago now stilled.

But she knew that the lives of the Lakota depended on so many things from the deer, so she had fought off her nausea and thanked Running Fox for his gift, for that was what it was considered when a husband brought home his kill for his wife.

Nancy's thoughts were interrupted and her heart warmed when she saw Running Fox take aim, then loose an arrow from his large and powerful bow.

The whooping from the men was enough for her to know that he had downed the animal and was even now rowing toward shore to make certain it was dead and not merely injured and lying there, suffering.

Just as Running Fox stepped from his beached canoe, Nancy heard something behind her.

Before she could turn and see what it was, a gag was suddenly tied around her mouth, silencing her.

Rough hands were on her arms, dragging her away from the cliff's edge. Then they turned her on her back, and her eyes went wide with shock when she looked up and the moon's glow revealed to her that the man who was now standing over her and holding her in place with a heavy foot on her belly was her stepfather!

Unable to speak because of the gag so tight around her mouth, and wrists quickly bound, Nancy was helpless.

But what was so shocking was that he had regained his faculties. She would never forget the blank look in his eyes the morning after his ordeal on the burial ground. Spittle had run from the corners of his mouth, and he did not respond to anything or anyone.

He had been taken away with the other mindless men and set free far from the Lakota village and Dry Gulch.

No one had expected ever to see them again. As far as Nancy and everyone else knew, the men had been frightened mindless that night.

But here her stepfather was, standing over her, his foot heavy on her belly, within which lay her precious baby in her womb.

She feared for her child's life even more than for her own.

The rough treatment, especially her stepfather pressing so hard into her belly with his boot, might cause her to lose the child.

She was again at the mercy of this crazed man after thinking that she had been freed of him forever.

"Now what's my pretty Naughty Nancy doin' out here all alone in the moonlight?" Joe said, his eyes revealing that he was no less crazy than before.

Nancy saw the disarray and filth of his clothes, the rough whiskers on his face.

"And look at you," he said. "You're still dressed like an Injun squaw, like the last time I saw you. You're a disgrace to the white community. If they saw you, they'd spit on you. You know how they feel about women who cavort with Injuns."

Nancy mumbled against the gag, but found speaking impossible.

She could feel pain in her belly now, but hoped it was only from the pressure of the foot pressed into it.

"Thought I'd be in the loony bin by now, didn't you?" Joe said, laughing insanely. "Well, as you can see, I ain't. I didn't go home after regaining my senses, not when I have you to tend to. I've stayed in hiding until the perfect moment to finally get my vengeance on Running Fox. As I see it, taking you from him is the best way possible—I saw how devoted he was to you. I'm taking you where no one will ever find you, then I'm going to bring the law down hard on the Lakota for what they did to me and my pals."

He snickered. "And you," he said. "I'm gonna tell them that you and your mother had been forced to stay as captives at the village, and when they see no signs of you at the village, I'll tell them that if they wanted to use some muscle, they could dig you up from the grave where Running Fox had planted you after killing you."

His insanity made Nancy shiver.

She had to find a way to get free!

But how?

It seemed that he finally had her exactly where he wanted her.

Soon she would be dead.

He leaned down closer to her face. "And how is my pretty wife, my Naughty Carole?" he said, again chuckling. "My, oh, my, I don't hear you answering me, Daughter." He laughed wickedly. "Cat got 'cher tongue or what?"

Nancy tried to kick him, but he was too far from her feet for her to be able to do so.

She lay there waiting for him to get past his ranting and raving, yet hoping he would continue for a while longer, for the more he talked, the louder he got.

It was apparent that he had forgotten the warriors who were hunting just below.

But then he seemed to remember. He looked over his shoulder toward the cliff's edge, then smiled cynically at Nancy again. "I almost forgot," he said. "The Lakota warriors are not that far away, are they? But none will come to your rescue. Why, they have no idea this whiskey peddler has captured the prime catch of the night. Won't your handsome chief miss you at night once I do away with you? You are one of the Lakota now, ain't you? You're sleeping with the chief."

He leaned low again, his eyes darkening. "Who is my wife sleeping with?" he growled.

Nancy's eyes widened when he placed a hand at her throat. After a moment he yanked it away again.

She tried to work herself free of his foot, but the more she squirmed, the harder he pressed it into her belly.

She was utterly helpless.

"Time's wastin'," Joe growled. "Once the hunt is over and the warriors return to their homes, you'll be missed. I need to take care of you proper-like before that. I don't want Running Fox to find me hiding you."

Nancy moaned against the gag when Joe grabbed

her long braid and began dragging her farther from the cliff and into the shadows of the forest.

As he dragged her along the ground, her scalp felt as though it were on fire.

Soon they were far from the torchlight and canoes.

Joe stopped and knelt down beside Nancy. "It seems like it's just the two of us again," he said, chuckling. "Now, let me see. What do you think I have planned for you? You'd like to be back home in the tepee, wouldn't you? Well, seems I've another lodge for you tonight."

Nancy's eyes widened as he glared at her, his eyes truly those of a madman.

She felt cold all over when he grabbed her arm and started dragging her toward the water. Now she feared that he was going to dump her into the lake, where she would drown. With her wrists tied, there was no way she could keep herself above water.

Yet he had said something about a lodge.

Where was it?

Why was he still dragging her toward the water?

"Got it figured out yet?" Joe taunted with a cackle.

Nancy's eyes met his, the moon's glow revealing his lunatic expression.

She was afraid that she was living her last moments on earth, and her heart cried out for Running Fox.

"Well, now I know you don't have any idea where I'm taking you, so I'll let you in on my little secret," Joe said, stepping into the water and dragging her behind him. "You know about muskrat houses, don't you? How they build them so's some of the house is made of twisted twigs, grass, and water plants cemented together with mud, and how these houses resemble in size and shape a cock of hay—how half is above water and the other half below it? Well, Naughty Nancy, that's where I'm putting you—in a muskrat house. I searched until I found one big enough for you, one that had enough air space that would last as long as it doesn't rain and raise the water level in the lake. I checked it out before I came for you. It's empty now."

He stopped for a moment, her full body in the water now except for her face. "Now there is another thing," he said. "The muskrats might not like having a new occupant in their house. They might just take out their anger on you. How long do you think they'd allow you to live once they tear into you?"

Nancy shuddered involuntarily at the gruesome possibilities.

The man was truly a lunatic for having devised this evil plan that would end in her losing her life in such a wicked way.

She tried to kick at him, but he just snickered and dodged her feet. Then he tied her into a fetal position so that she would not be able to free herself and get out of the muskrat house. He then shoved her head down into the water long enough to push her into the dwelling.

Nancy's heart beat rapidly inside her chest when her mouth and nose surfaced and she could breathe again.

A cold fear spread through her. She was shoved in so tightly that she couldn't budge.

All that was above the water was her face, from her chin up.

Thank God the animals weren't there, at least not at this moment. If they were out tonight scavenging for food, they would be gone for a while.

"Naughty Nancy, because of you and that flea-bitten Indian-chief lover of yours, I've lost everything—my theater, my supply of whiskey, everything," she could hear Joe say as he knelt down over the muskrat house. "But I'll get it all back. When I make my reappearance and tell them the story about how me and my men were abducted and taken to Ghost Island, and then about how you were killed by the savage, and how they still held your mother captive, the law will come down hard on your Injun friends. And when your mother contradicts what I tell the lawmen, I'll just call her a liar. They'll believe me over her anytime."

There was a strained silence, and then Joe said, "Yep, you are the one to pay for what happened to me."

Then everything became eerily still.

Nancy gazed down at the water, knowing that if it did rain, or if the tide came up at all, she would die a terrible death by drowning.

Terrified, she thought of the muskrats.

What would their reaction be to first seeing her there, crowding their space with her body?

Chapter 33

Neither Nancy nor Joseph Brock had seen eyes watching all that was happening, nor did Nancy hear the patter of little feet as this child ran hard toward her home to tell her mother what she had just seen, and about where Nancy was imprisoned!

Tiny Doe owed Nancy a debt for having given her back her eyesight with the aid of the eyeglasses!

Tiny Doe was going to do more than that for Nancy now.

She was going to save her life!

Breathing hard, Tiny Doe ran up to her tepee shouting, "*Ina*, Mother! Mother! Come quickly! Nancy! She is in trouble!"

Her mother hurried outside. She knelt down and held her daughter at arm's length, gazing into the little girl's fearful eyes.

"Tiny Doe, I did not know you were gone," she said, her voice breaking. "Not until now, not until I heard your voice and you awakened me from my sleep. I was resting before your *ahte*, father, comes home with a deer, for I will work the rest of the night preparing it. And what is this you said about Nancy? She should be in her lodge, too, awaiting Running Fox's arrival."

"She is not there," Tiny Doe said, finally able to get her breath. "Oh, *Ina*, I did something you will not like, but had I not, I would not have seen Nancy abducted by that evil man and placed in a muskrat's house at the edge of the lake."

Morning Flower gasped. Her fingers tightened on her daughter's shoulders. "What did you just say?" she gasped out. "Where did you say Nancy was?"

"*Ina*, there is not much time," Tiny Doe cried, sobbing now and worried that Nancy was not going to live. She loved her so much.

"We must go and tell Chief Running Fox," Morning Flower said, sweeping Tiny Doe up into her arms and running with her toward the warriors in their canoes.

"But we should not go near where the arrows are being shot from the canoes," Tiny Doe fretted. "*Ina*, I am afraid."

"When I get close enough I will shout at the men to stop firing and then I will tell Running Fox what you saw," Morning Flower said, still holding tight to Tiny Doe as she ran onward in the moonlight. "Tell me, Tiny Doe. Tell me everything so that I can then relay the same to our chief."

"I wanted to see the hunt from the canoes even though I know I was told I should not be near there," Tiny Doe said, clinging to her mother's neck as she continued to run, now along the shore. "Now that I can see, I want to see everything. I stayed far enough away not to be accidentally shot by an arrow. But I saw something else. I saw Nancy being dragged by the hair by the evil whiskey man. I saw where he took Nancy. He tied her up and put her in a muskrat house, Mother, then left. I don't know how to swim and I am afraid of muskrats, so I knew that I could not help Nancy myself. I knew that you would know what to do."

"Although you were very wrong not to listen to what both me and your *ahte* told you about the dangers of being near the deer hunt, I am glad that you witnessed our chief's wife being abducted and especially that you saw where she was taken," Morning Flower said. "Tiny Doe, you are a very brave little girl."

"Nancy gave me eyes, so I hope I can give her back her life by helping save her tonight," Tiny Doe said. Then her mother slid her from her arms and knelt before Tiny Doe. "I cannot take you any farther. It is dangerous. Stay here. I will call to Running Fox, then come back for you," Morning Flower said. She hurried away, shouting Running Fox's name over and over again.

Running Fox heard.

His heart skipped a beat when he heard Morning Flower's frantic tone. "Stop the hunt!" he shouted to his men, then rowed toward shore, afraid to hear what had brought the woman into danger tonight by coming for him.

Chapter 34

Running Fox stopped short when he saw not only Morning Flower but also Tiny Doe, who was with her mother again, clutching her mother's hand and looking anxiously up at him through her eyeglasses.

"What brings you here in such a frantic way?" Running Fox asked, holding his torch closer to Morning Flower's face and seeing the stark terror in her eyes. "Why have you brought your daughter? You know the dangers of being this close to where the deer hunt is being held."

"Tiny Doe had not been able to see much in her lifetime before she was given the spectacles by your wife," Morning Flower told him urgently. "That is why she disobeyed me and came to watch the hunt by torchlight. It sounded exciting to her."

"But she could have been killed," Running Fox

said, kneeling to look directly into Tiny Doe's eyes. "You did know the dangers—yet you came."

"Yes, but I am so glad that I did," Tiny Doe said, a sob lodging in her throat. "Had I not, I could not have seen Nancy being dragged away by her hair by that evil whiskey man."

Running Fox felt as though someone had poured ice water over him, for the shock of what he had just heard was so severe.

It could not be true.

He had seen the blankness in Joseph Brock's eyes when he had been released along with the other mindless men.

"You should not make up such stories that frighten your chief," Running Fox said gravely. He stood up and gazed into Morning Flower's eyes. "You have much to teach your daughter about obedience and about telling false tales."

He pointed in the direction of their village. "Take her home," he said flatly. "I will have to talk with her later in the presence of both you and her father. She must never do anything like this again. Someone could have died."

"Nancy will die if you do not go and take her from the muskrat's home," Tiny Doe said, sobbing. She wiped at the tears as they streamed down her cheeks. "I—I—did see that evil man drag her from the cliff, tie her up, then take her and shove her into the muskrat house. I could not help her. I am too small. That is why I went for my mother. I knew she would know what to do."

Suddenly Running Fox was aware that this child was too small to imagine anything as vivid as she had described. If what she said was true, Nancy was in terrible jeopardy.

"What you are saying is true, is it not?" Running Fox said, again kneeling before Tiny Doe.

"It is true and I am afraid for Nancy," Tiny Doe gulped. "She has been so kind to me. Because of her I can now see more than movement and shadow. I can truly see everything. I saw her being taken away and then shoved into that muskrat house."

The very thought of his Nancy being accosted in such a way and then placed in a muskrat house, of all things, made Running Fox's insides burn with such hate for the whiskey man that it was hard to control himself.

"Where is the man who put her there?" he asked, ready to kill the man at first sight.

"He left," Tiny Doe said. "I do not know where he went because I needed to come and get my mother so that she could get help in getting Nancy from that horrible place."

"I will worry about him later," Running Fox said, standing tall, his eyes glittering in the light of the torch's glow. "You can take me to Nancy, can you not?"

"Yes, but please hurry," Tiny Doe said, another sob catching in her throat.

"I shall alert my men, and then you must lead me to her," Running Fox said, running back in the direction of the men waiting in their canoes.

When he reached the embankment, he held his torch high. "Beach your canoes," he shouted. "Come with me. My wife is in danger."

Everyone did as he commanded, and soon Tiny Doe was in Running Fox's arms, pointing the way to where Nancy was imprisoned.

When they got close enough to see the muskrat house at the edge of the water, Tiny Doe cried as she pointed it out to Running Fox.

"She is there!" she sobbed. "Nancy is there!"

Running Fox thrust his torch into Gray Raven's hand and ran into the water.

He tore away the thick, twisted branches and twigs, soon uncovering Nancy, whose eyes were red and swollen from crying, and whose mouth was still gagged.

Nancy had hardly believed her ears when she had heard Running Fox's voice as well as Tiny Doe's, and now, as he reached down inside the muskrat house, she almost collapsed completely, for her fear had taken a dreadful toll on her.

Running Fox yanked the gag from her mouth, and his eyes searched hers as Gray Raven held the torch closer. "My woman," Running Fox said, his voice breaking. "The light of my life. How could anyone have done this to you?"

"He is very much alive and alert," Nancy said through her sobs. "He—he—left me here to die, and then you were to be next."

Running Fox yanked his knife from its sheath at his right side and sliced the ropes at her wrists and ankles, finally releasing her from her bonds.

"I have found his tracks!" Running Fox's best tracker cried, dashing up to him. "They are easily identified as they make their way through the dew-covered grass. I believe he was headed toward a cave that I am aware of. He has surely made it his home as he awaited the opportune time to do what he did tonight."

"He will never do anything else," Running Fox solemnly pronounced.

He twined his arms around Nancy's waist, drew her close, and brushed soft kisses across her lips, then stepped away from her, his eyes devouring her.

"You always said you wanted a role in his come-uppance," he said gravely. "Come. You will have that opportunity tonight, and tonight will be the last time we will have to concern ourselves about that man again. I will not leave anything to chance this time. He will die!"

Nancy swallowed hard, wiped renewed tears from her eyes, then nodded. "Yes, we shouldn't risk allowing him to be free to wreak any more havoc.

He plans to lie about everything, to make it look as though he was the wronged person. He plans to bring the lawmen into your village, to take what is left of your people's dignity."

"He is a man of evil," Running Fox said harshly. "He must have been allowed by your God to live for some reason, but I cannot think of any good enough reason that this should have been granted. It is just by chance that he still lives. After tonight, that chance will have run out. I will make certain this time that when I walk away from him, he will have breathed his last breath of life."

He turned to Morning Flower, who held Tiny Doe in her arms. "Thank you for all that you have done for me tonight. I shall never forget it." He reached a gentle hand to Tiny Doe's face. "You did wrong tonight, but it turned into something very right. *Hiye-pila-maya*, thank you, Tiny Doe."

Tiny Doe nodded and giggled.

Running Fox turned back to Morning Flower. "Go home," he said gently. "Your job is done here and—and thank you. Had you not come and alerted me about this horrible deed, my woman, my wife, might not have survived."

Nancy went to Morning Flower and Tiny Doe and embraced them both at the same time. "I shall never forget this," she said, then jumped with alarm when she saw glittering eyes in the dark coming her way, knowing it was the family of muskrats returning to their home.

Had she been there these next few moments, she had no idea how the muskrats would have treated her.

"I will leave now," Morning Flower said, carrying Tiny Doe in the direction of their village.

Running Fox smiled at Nancy. "My *mitawin*, let us go and find us a villain of villains," he said. "Let us show him that he did not hide you well enough."

Nancy shivered from being so cold, but there was no time to go for blankets.

They had already wasted too much time in talking.

Running Fox went to his canoe and grabbed his bow and quiver of arrows, as the others equipped themselves with the same.

They then fell into step behind the tracker.

"The cave is not that far away," the scout said, only loud enough for Running Fox to hear. "It is certain now that is where he has gone. The tracks will lead us directly there."

Running Fox nodded.

Nancy cringed.

They walked onward for a while longer. Then Running Fox stopped and turned to his warriors. "We must put the fire out on the torches," he said quietly. One by one the flames were extinguished.

They then proceeded stealthily to the cave, which was known as an old bear haunt.

A campfire could be seen just inside the cave, the smoke weaving in slow spirals out of the entrance.

Running Fox turned to Nancy. "I should go in first, alone."

"You said that I could have a role in his comeuppance, so please don't ask me not to," Nancy asked, pleading with her eyes. The moon's glow revealed this to Running Fox. "Please?"

"Yes, come with me," Running Fox said, knowing that it would be asking a lot of her not to allow her to go with him. "But you have no weapon."

Nancy glanced down at the huge knife that was belted at his waist, then smiled up at him. "Your knife," she said.

He hesitated, then gave it to her. "I hope you do not get close enough to him to have to use it."

"No matter what, we must stop him tonight, forever," Nancy said resolutely.

Running Fox nodded.

He turned to his warriors. "Surround the entrance of the cave," he said. "Keep your bowstrings notched with arrows. If he tries to escape, kill him immediately."

The warriors nodded and prepared their arrows. Running Fox notched an arrow onto his own string.

He glanced at Nancy, smiled, then moved silently

onward. They could now see Joe sitting beside the fire, a jug of whiskey lifted to his lips.

He had managed to steal some whiskey from someone, and by the way he teetered as he sat, it was obvious that he was quite drunk.

As Running Fox moved closer, he stepped on a twig, which snapped loudly. Joe dropped the jug and leapt to his feet.

He grabbed for his rifle, yanked it up, and just as he aimed it at Nancy an arrow was loosed from Running Fox's bowstring and found its home in the evil man's heart, the impact of the arrow causing Joe to drop his rifle as he fell to the rocky floor of the cave.

He lay lifeless beside the fire, his eyes locked in a death stare. Nancy went inside the cave, for she had to see for certain, herself, that this evil man was finally dead.

She stared at him, still finding it hard to believe that her stepfather would hate her so much that he would leave her in that terrible muskrat house to die by drowning, exposure, or muskrat bites.

Suddenly all of the warriors crowded inside the cave to see for themselves this time if the man was truly dead.

One warrior approached Nancy.

He had gone back to the canoes and had gotten a blanket, which he now slid around Nancy's shoulders.

She thanked him and hugged it to her, then turned to Running Fox. "Joe did something else tonight that might end in tragedy," she said, her voice breaking.

He placed his hands at her waist and drew her close, their eyes meeting and holding. "What are you talking about?"

She explained how Joe had held his foot so tightly on her belly and how she feared it might have harmed the child inside her womb.

"What if he did?" Nancy said, searching his eyes. "It would give him the vengeance that he sought tonight."

Running Fox gently embraced her. "My *mitawin*, we must place all of this behind us now, even the fear that came with what he did. I believe in good always overcoming evil, even if it must be fought for. When our child is born to us, you will see that no Great Spirit or your white man's God would allow our child to be harmed because of this man's great evil."

Nancy twined her arms around his neck and clung to him. "You always make things so right inside my heart. I know now that I was foolish to worry about our child. I will not think about such concerns any longer. In time we will be able to look back on this and even smile."

"We must go home now and tell your *ina* about what happened," Running Fox said. "We can give her peace of mind when she learns that Joe is dead."

"She will be relieved to know that the nightmare that started for her when she met Joseph Brock is finally, truly, over," Nancy said, smiling grimly. "As is mine."

Chapter 35

In the Moon of the Changing Seasons—October

It was another autumn, and groves of cottonwood trees stood stately and tall, their foliage fast turning yellow, in striking contrast to the brilliant scarlet of the sarvis berry and wild roses.

Many leaves had fallen, exposing the silver gray of the cottonwood trunks and revealing the delicate purple of the alder bushes and the bright red branches of the thickets and willows.

Running Fox sat on mats on the floor of his lodge, carving a new bow, casting occasional proud glances over at Nancy as she sat close by, in the warmth of the fire, singing to their baby daughter and rocking her back and forth in her arms, while the baby suckled from Nancy's milk-filled breast.

"Our daughter," Running Fox said, setting his bow and carving knife aside. He crawled over and sat beside Nancy. "Our little Pretty Sun."

He bent low and brushed a soft kiss across Nancy's breast just above where their daughter's nose was pressed into her flesh, her tiny lips wrapped around the dark nipple.

"This is a beautiful moment," Running Fox said. "There are so many such as this with you and our baby. She is such a tiny, beautiful thing." He smiled into Nancy's eyes. "As beautiful as her mother."

"I am so content, Running Fox," Nancy murmured. "Sometimes it scares me. I have had so much happiness stolen from me in my past, and I am not certain what I would do if something or someone did that to me again."

"Worrying about such things is wasted energy. Do you not know that?" Running Fox said, weaving his fingers through her long black hair, which was hanging loose and free down her back. "All is well between our Fox Band and the whites in the area, as well as among us and the Chippewa."

"Ah, yes, the Chippewa," Nancy said, laughing softly. "I would have never guessed that things could happen so quickly as they have between my mother and Chief Winter Moon."

Just as she said that, a familiar voice wafted into the tepee.

Running Fox went to the entrance flap and

swept it aside, smiling when he saw Carole running to meet Winter Moon as he came from his beached canoe.

"I believe we might have another wedding ceremony on our hands one of these days," Running Fox said. "Winter Moon has arrived for another, as you call it, 'picnic' today with your mother. She has the basket with her as she meets him. He is being introduced to foods even I have not yet been introduced to."

"That is because before my mother met Joe Brock, she loved to cook," Nancy said, gazing at their child, realizing she had fallen asleep when she stopped suckling from her breast.

She gently drew Pretty Sun away from the breast, closed the flap made in the dress especially for nursing, then rose and took Pretty Sun to her cradle, which Running Fox had made for her.

Nancy laid a soft blanket of doeskin across the baby, so that only her face was open to the light, then joined Running Fox to spy on two people in love.

"Today Mama has made an apple pie for Winter Moon from the apples recently picked in the forest," she told him. "I smelled the pie baking early this morning. It is amazing how she managed to make an oven that works in the coals of the lodge fire so that she can make not only her pies but also delicious bread and biscuits."

"She has made the same for you," Running Fox said, dropping the entrance flap and turning to place his hands gently at her waist. "But I have not yet seen any pies or biscuits."

"I am always so afraid I will disappoint. I just can't seem to master cooking," Nancy said almost shyly. "Does that matter? Do I disappoint you?"

"You never disappoint," Running Fox said softly. "Where you are weak in some things that you do, you are better at others." He glanced over at the bed of blankets, and then into Nancy's eyes. "I believe you know what I mean."

"Shall we test that theory now?" Nancy teased, running a finger across his lips. "Pretty Sun will be asleep for some time."

"Nancy? Running Fox?"

Her mother's voice speaking from outside the tepee made Nancy giggle, for she knew that their "test" would have to come later.

Her mother had said that before she and Winter Moon went into the forest for a picnic, she wanted to share some of the pie with Nancy and Running Fox. She knew just how much Running Fox loved the pie, as well as the continued camaraderie with Chief Winter Moon.

Each time they came together, their friendship was strengthened.

Sharing pie was one of the best ways of enjoying one's company.

"I believe Mama wants you to have some pie and some moments with Winter Moon before they go and have time alone," Nancy murmured.

"Then we shall have pie," Running Fox said, holding the entrance flap aside for Carole and Winter Moon.

Nancy grabbed his hand, stopping him.

She leaned closer to him, gazing lovingly into his eyes. "My handsome chieftain husband, I'll never be able to tell you enough times how much I love you," she said softly. "Oh, how I do adore you."

Running Fox swept her close and kissed her, but they were drawn apart quickly again when Carole again spoke their name through the closed flap.

Nancy giggled. "She has always been a persistent one."

Running Fox paused for a moment longer as he gazed into Nancy's violet eyes. "My *mitawin*, everything is good," he said huskily.

"My husband, everything is wonderful," Nancy said, then stood beside Running Fox as he finally held the entrance flap aside for the powerful Chippewa chief and the woman whom Nancy was so proud to call her *ina*.

"Well, hello, you two," Carole said, beaming as she held the pie out toward Running Fox. "I hope we didn't interrupt something."

"No, you didn't—nor could you ever," Nancy said, stepping farther back into the tepee as Winter

Moon came inside with Carole, a broad smile for Nancy warming her heart, for she would never forget those first moments with him when he had made her so uneasy with his coldness.

Now she knew that he was one of the warmest-hearted men she had ever known. Were his skin white, she would believe it was her father reincarnated—they were so much alike in personality.

"Plates, Nancy," Carole said, already slicing the pie. "I think this is the best I ever baked."

Nancy laughed softly, for she recalled that her mother had always said that same thing every time she made a pie, back when her life was centered around house, husband, and daughter.

It was so good to have her mother back again—the true mother she had known before Joseph Brock came into their lives.

"And how is the beautiful daughter?" Winter Moon asked as he went and stood over the cradle.

"She is growing more each day," Nancy said, smiling at Running Fox, seeing that he was watching her every movement with such a look of love in his dark, wonderful eyes.

She blushed when he silently mouthed the words "I love you" to her in his Lakota language, both knowing that once the pie was eaten and the older lovebirds had left, Running Fox and Nancy's stolen moments would be theirs to enjoy while Pretty Sun slept contentedly close by them.

Dear Reader:

I hope you enjoyed reading *Running Fox*. The next book in my Dreamcatcher series, written exclusively for NAL/Signet, is *Shadow Bear*. It is filled with much excitement, romance, mystery, and adventure. *Shadow Bear* will be in stores in July 2007.

Many of you say that you are collecting my Indian romances. For my entire backlist of books, or for information about my fan club, you can send for my latest newsletter and autographed bookmark. For a personal reply from me, please send a stamped, self-addressed, legal-size envelope to:

Cassie Edwards
6709 N. Country Club Road
Mattoon, Illinois 61938

Thank you for your support of my new Dreamcatcher series. I love researching and writing about our Native Americans. I aspire to write about every major tribe in America.

Always,

Cassie Edwards
www.cassieedwards.com

New York Times bestselling author

Madeline Baker

Under Apache Skies
0-451-21282-7

When a rugged stranger darkens the door of her
family porch, Martha Jean Flynn can tell right
away that Ridge Longtree is nothing like the other
cowboys who usually show up in search of work.
But when tragedy strikes, Marty must flee with the
half-Indian loner—and she discovers a love that
threatens to set her heart aflame.

Dakota Dreams
0-451-21686-5

Nathan Chasing Elk was looking for his lost
daughter—and to avenge the death of his wife.
Catharine Lyons was struggling to maintain her
ranch when Nathan stumbled onto her property,
badly injured. Together they would try to mend
their lives—and discover a passion neither has
ever known.

**Available wherever books are sold or at
penguin.com**

S903

Penguin Group (USA) Online

What will you be reading tomorrow?

Tom Clancy, Patricia Cornwell, W.E.B. Griffin,
Nora Roberts, William Gibson, Robin Cook,
Brian Jacques, Catherine Coulter, Stephen King,
Dean Koontz, Ken Follett, Clive Cussler,
Eric Jerome Dickey, John Sandford,
Terry McMillan, Sue Monk Kidd, Amy Tan,
John Berendt...

You'll find them all at
penguin.com

*Read excerpts and newsletters,
find tour schedules and reading group guides,
and enter contests.*

Subscribe to Penguin Group (USA) newsletters
and get an exclusive inside look
at exciting new titles and the authors you love
long before everyone else does.

PENGUIN GROUP (USA)
us.penguingroup.com